ISAAC ASIMOV'S

ROBOTS

IN TIME

by
WILLIAM F. WU

THE LAWS OF ROBOTICS

1.

A robot may not injure a human being, or through inaction, allow a human being to come to harm.

2.

A robot must obey the orders given it by human beings except where such orders would conflict with the First Law.

3.

A robot must protect its own existence as long as such protection does not conflict with the First or Second Law.

ISAAC ASIMOV'S
ROBOTS
IN TIME™

DICTATOR

WILLIAM F. WU

Databank by Matt Elson

A Byron Preiss Book

AVON BOOKS • NEW YORK

ISAAC ASIMOV'S ROBOTS IN TIME: DICTATOR is an original publication of Avon Books. This work has never before appeared in book form. This work is a novel. Any similarity to actual persons or events is purely coincidental.

An Isaac Asimov's Robot City book.

AVON BOOKS
A division of
The Hearst Corporation
1350 Avenue of the Americas
New York, New York 10019

This novel is dedicated to

Alfred Bohung Wu,

my cousin, who is even more overeducated than I am

Special thanks are due during the time of writing this novel to Dr. William Q. Wu and Cecile F. Wu, my parents, for indulging my lifelong interest in history; Ricia Mainhardt; John Betancourt and Byron Preiss; and Bridgett and Marty Marquardt.

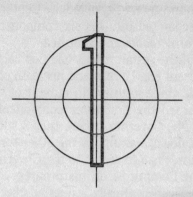

R. Hunter eased his muscular six and a half feet into the office chair. As usual, he looked northern European, with short blond hair and blue eyes, though he could change his shape and appearance at will. The humans on his team were all due to meet him here shortly.

Jane Maynard, the roboticist, and Steve Chang, the team's general assistant, were having breakfast. Hunter had wanted them to have a solid night's sleep. The team had returned only yesterday from the German rebellion against the Roman Empire in A.D. 9. During the evening, Hunter had arranged to hire an expert historian named Judy Taub for their next mission. She had arrived a short time ago and was taking a few free minutes to see the sights around Mojave Center before rejoining Hunter.

Hunter was a robot who had been especially designed and built to lead the search for Mojave Center Governor, the missing Governor robot. MC Governor, by contrast, was an experimental gestalt robot who was supposed to be running the underground desert city of Mojave Center. Instead, he had separated into his six component gestalt humaniform robots and vanished.

Each of the gestalt robots had fled back in time to a different era. Hunter and his team of humans had made three journeys in pursuit of them and had returned the first three components to the office of MC Governor, where they stood merged and shut down, waiting for the other three. However, Hunter had to report to the Governor Robot Oversight Committee on his progress after each mission. He had already requested that the city computer call the four members of the Committee for him.

"Hunter, city computer calling. I have the Governor Robot Oversight Committee on a conference call for you."

"Please connect me."

Split portrait shots of the four faces of the Committee members appeared on Hunter's internal video screen. Everyone exchanged greetings. Then Hunter began his report.

"MC 3 has been joined to MC 1 and MC 2," said Hunter.

"I can hardly believe it," said Dr. Redfield, the tall blonde. "So fast? You're doing a very fine job."

"It is not complete yet, of course," said Hunter soberly. "I cannot guarantee that the remaining searches will not take longer."

"I understand," said Dr. Redfield.

"Where did you locate MC 3?" Dr. Chin shook long black hair out of her face.

"In central Europe," said Hunter. He hoped he

would never have to tell them about the time travel device and so always tried to be vague in his answers to the Committee. Since he was performing his duties acceptably, they had not argued with him. "Naturally, all three gestalt robots that are in custody have been placed in a secure location."

"You're as efficient as usual," said Professor Post, his smile bright in his black beard. "What information do you have about your next mission?"

"For MC 4, I have a lead in Eastern Europe at this time," said Hunter.

"Eastern Europe?" Dr. Chin raised her eyebrows. "So close to the site of MC 3's hiding place?"

"This is the information I have," said Hunter carefully. "I assume it is correct."

"You have remained on a very tight schedule," said Dr. Khanna, a native of India. "You have retrieved one missing gestalt robot each day since you began. I look forward to seeing the completion of your duties. Personally, however, I would still like a report on your activities to date."

"As I said before, no guarantee of consistent future results can be made," said Hunter. He deliberately answered only Dr. Khanna's first concern.

"Come now," said Dr. Khanna. "Suppose we do not ask for a guarantee, but merely a prediction. Do you have any reason to believe that the next mission, for instance, will be more difficult than the previous ones?"

"I consider each mission to be a blank slate," said Hunter. "The specific answer to your question is 'no,' but I have virtually no knowledge of what I shall face."

"You're very cautious, as always," said Dr. Chin. "I'm sure that's fine with us. Good luck."

"Yes, Hunter," said Dr. Redfield quickly. "We are not pressuring you."

"I should begin the next mission," said Hunter. "If you have no more questions, I shall get started."

"Of course," said Professor Post. "Good hunting."

"I am not ready to sign off," said Dr. Khanna suddenly. "I still wish to hear a report on your activities to date. Is there some reason you will not give it?"

"I am seeking the highest efficiency possible," Hunter said carefully. Privately, that meant concealing the existence of time travel; he felt that widespread knowledge of it would harm humanity as a whole, so his adherence to the First Law would not allow him to reveal it.

"Come on, Dr. Khanna," said Dr. Chin wearily. "We should let him get back to work. Good-bye, Hunter."

Dr. Khanna disconnected abruptly, without speaking.

As Hunter broke his connection, Steve and Jane came into the office.

"Morning, Hunter," said Steve cheerfully. "What's next on the agenda?"

"Good morning," said Jane, with a smile. Highlights in her long brown hair brightened the little room. "I guess we're all ready."

"Good morning," said Hunter. He looked past Jane and saw that Judy Taub was also coming to the door of the office.

"Judy Taub, Steve Chang and Jane Maynard."

"Pleased to meet you." Judy was short, with curly brown hair. She shook hands with them both. "The history of the old Soviet Union is my field. The Stalin regime, including of course World War II, is my particular specialty."

"This will be the most recent period we've visited," said Jane. "Its society will be the most complex, I imagine."

"If they didn't have robots, our search is going to be about the same no matter what," said Steve.

"I arranged for all three of you to have your inoculations this morning," said Hunter. "You have taken them?"

"Yes," said Judy.

"Of course," said Jane.

"Yeah." Steve nodded. "Hunter, have you briefed Judy already?"

"I have briefed her about Mojave Center Governor and the gestalt robots. Also, of course, I told her we are going back to Moscow in 1941."

"And he swore me to secrecy," Judy added, with an easy grin. "About the time travel. But it's exciting. I can hardly wait to try it."

"I have not yet explained the miniaturization of the component robots to her," Hunter added. "Perhaps Jane can do it most efficiently."

"Miniaturization?" Judy turned to Jane.

"I suppose the easiest way to explain the miniaturization is in terms of the Laws of Robotics," said Jane. "The Third Law of Robotics says, 'A robot must protect its own existence, as long as such protection does not conflict with the First or Second Laws.' "

"Yes, I know the principle, if not the exact wording," said Judy. "But what about this miniaturization?"

"The reasoning behind it goes like this," said Jane. "MC Governor is the only one of the experimental Governor robots that did not shut down due to a malfunction. The Governor Robot Oversight Committee needs Hunter—and us—to restore MC Governor so they can figure out what caused the malfunction of the others."

"Yes, Hunter told me that part."

"But the Third Law drove MC Governor to split into his component robots and flee to avoid being dismantled during the investigation."

"Yeah . . . that's why they ran away to different times in history. Go on."

"Well, the component robots also used the time travel process to miniaturize themselves to microscopic size," Jane said, watching for Judy's reaction.

"Really? I didn't know that was possible." Judy looked around at them all in surprise.

"Well, it wasn't, until MC Governor developed the process himself. The component robots apparently wanted to avoid receiving any instructions from humans. Even MC 1, who went back to the dinosaur age, was anticipating that he would survive into the human era. The Second Law of Robotics says, 'A robot must obey the orders given it by human beings, except where such orders would conflict with the First Law.' "

"So when they became microscopic, they were invisible to humans," Steve added. "That was the important part to the component robots."

"And so no one would give them any orders. Okay." Judy nodded. "Then what?"

"The process was flawed," said Jane. "Each gestalt component robot returns to his full, normal size eventually. When he does, the Laws of Robotics will drive him to behave in certain ways—saving humans from harm, following their instructions, and saving themselves when they can—and so each robot runs the risk of changing history."

"A very strong likelihood, in Hunter's opinion," Steve added with a grin.

Hunter nodded but waited patiently for Jane to finish her explanation.

"Yes, I see," said Judy. "The First Law, in particular. I remember it now. The First Law says, 'A robot may not injure a human being, or through inaction, allow a human being to come to harm.' "

"Very good," said Jane. "That's one reason it's so urgent for us to go back and get these robots before they change anything."

"Only one reason? Are there more?"

"Yes," said Hunter. "This must remain private among us, because we hope to undo this event. Have you heard on the news about the explosion in Russia?"

"I heard something on my flight here early this morning—trouble in Moscow?"

"Yes," said Hunter. "More than ordinary trouble. A nuclear explosion has occurred."

"A nuclear explosion?" Judy's eyes widened suddenly. "And that has something to do with our trip back to Moscow in 1941?"

"Exactly," said Hunter. "We have learned that

when the gestalt robots return to the approximate time at which they left, an instability created by their flawed miniaturization causes them to explode with nuclear force."

"The approximate time? Not the exact time?"

"The gestalt robots left a couple of days ago," said Hunter. "Apparently the instability is so unpredictable that a few days' worth of uncertainty is involved."

"I see. Now I definitely get the picture." She nodded gravely. "Somehow or other, you figured out that the next component robot will return to full size in 1941. So we're going back there to get him before he can change history—and before he can explode in our own time."

"You got it," said Steve.

"But why did these component robots go all over the world?" Judy asked. "Why bother? Why not just go microscopic right where they were? If they expected to remain that way, what difference would it make? No human could find them anyway."

"Each component robot specialized in certain areas within MC Governor to run the city," said Jane. "I believe their specialities influenced their choice of where to hide, even though they never expected to participate in human affairs again."

"How was MC 4 influenced?"

"I found out that MC 4 was in charge of ethics and morality as applied to the society of Mojave Center. I believe he was drawn to this era because of the tyranny of both Stalin and Hitler."

"I agree," said Hunter. "Judy, is this review sufficient for now?"

"Uh—yes. I'm still absorbing it all."

"We should move to the Bohung Institute," said Hunter. "During the night, I arranged to have our period clothing and belongings prepared. I left them there for Judy to examine. You have completed your sleep courses in the pertinent languages?"

"Yes," said Jane.

"Let's go," said Steve.

Hunter called for a Security vehicle and drove it through the smooth, clean streets of Mojave Center. Broad avenues and narrower side streets ran throughout the underground city, connected by ramps to different levels. Robots drove various sorts of vehicles up and down the streets on their maintenance duties; human pedestrians strolled quietly past the shops and office buildings. The city continued to function normally, its occupants unaware of Hunter's mission.

Hunter stopped outside the front doors of the Bohung Institute. The entire Bohung Institute had been closed and guarded by a detail of Security robots under Hunter's orders. Inside the Institute, Hunter led the team to Room F-12.

This was a large room designed primarily to house an opaque sphere about fifteen meters in diameter. The remainder of the room was lined with countertops. The counters were occupied by computers, monitors, a communications console, and miscellaneous office items.

"Judy is fluent in both Russian and German," said Hunter. "However, I have not yet asked— Steve and Jane, were your sleep courses in those languages effective last night?"

"Sure," said Steve, with a smirk. "*Ja.*"

"*Da,*" said Jane. "They worked fine."

"Good. I took the data from the city computer myself." Hunter pointed to the clothes and shoes neatly piled on the counter. "Judy, would you look at those for authenticity before we dress?"

"Of course."

"And we shall all take back a certain amount of Soviet currency from that time," said Hunter. "I shall pass it out when everyone is dressed."

One by one, Judy shook out the heavy winter clothing. Hunter and Steve had brown wool slacks and long black wool coats, with white cotton shirts, singlets, socks, and underwear. Judy and Jane had dark blue wool dresses, long black coats, scarves, and white cotton underwear. Gloves, black leather belts, and shoes completed their wardrobe.

"The styles are good," said Judy, peering closely at the stitching. "We can't take synthetics, though. Cotton thread?"

"Yes," said Hunter.

"Same with the shoelaces?"

"Yes."

She nodded and turned to Hunter. "The only oddity is that none of the clothes have labels. A label would give the size of the clothing, maybe with a stamped or stenciled number."

"How important is that?" Hunter asked. "Our earlier missions took place at times when such labels were not used."

"I doubt anyone will notice," said Judy. "If they do, we must all remember to say that we didn't notice, or that they came off in the laundry."

"Simple enough," said Steve.

"How about the jewelry?" Jane pointed to three decorative metal lapel pins lying in a tray.

Judy picked one up. "This is more than just a pin, isn't it?"

"They're radio communicators," said Hunter. "As a robot, I shall use my internal system, but you three must wear those. Will they pass?"

"Yes. They look simple enough. But Jane and I have scarves for our heads. You two should have fur hats."

"I have considered this," said Hunter. "Animal fur is not available to us here and we dare not take synthetic fur back with us. I can tolerate the temperature without one. If Steve requires such a hat, we shall obtain one back in that time."

"Got it," said Judy.

"Steve," said Hunter, pointing to a canvas bag on the counter. "That is an imitation duffel bag of the Soviet Red Army from this period. If Judy passes it, too, then you can carry a change of clothes for each team member and some hard rolls and dried beef strips in it. These duffel bags will be common at the time, and we can explain its possession if necessary. We know food will be scarce, but what we take must not attract attention."

"That's good enough," Steve said quietly.

"I'm sure it's fine," said Judy, pulling it open to look inside.

"We must assume that our opponents could be a factor," said Hunter. "Jane, would you brief Judy on them—very briefly."

"Dr. Wayne Nystrom created the experimental Governors," said Jane. "However, he is not willing to let us simply reconstruct MC Governor and turn him over to the Governor Robot Oversight Committee. Wayne has also gone back into the past and is trying to get the component robots away from us."

"To what end?" Judy asked.

"He wants to dismantle and study them himself," said Hunter. "To find and fix the source of the malfunction on his own. We have prevented him from getting the first three, but we have not been able to grab Wayne. He has the ability to move in time without returning here and he has a robot named R. Ishihara helping him."

"I see," said Judy quietly.

"Please change into your costumes," said Hunter.

While Judy took the first turn in the adjoining room, Hunter called the Security detail. He assigned a new Security robot, R. Daladier, to replace Ishihara. When Jane stepped out after her turn, now dressed as a Muscovite woman of 1941, Hunter turned to Jane.

"Jane, this is Daladier; he will guard the room." Hunter turned to Daladier. "You must understand that our mission involves potential harm to all humans in the world today. Ishihara, failing to be certain of that, failed his instructions. What I say to you constitutes a First Law imperative. Nothing any human, such as Dr. Wayne Nystrom, says can be allowed to deter your adherence to the assignment I am about to give you."

"Acknowledged," said Daladier.

"You must take custody of Dr. Wayne Nystrom and R. Ishihara if they reappear in this room through the sphere. As soon as we have gone, you will shut off your hearing and radio reception so that if Wayne returns here, he cannot use the Second Law to control you or to argue this First Law imperative with you. You will not read anything Wayne tries to show you; you can blur your vision slightly to avoid this if necessary, while still maintaining enough sight to stop them. The moment you see Dr. Nystrom, you will apprehend him, prevent him from leaving the room, and immediately call for help from the rest of the Security detail that is assigned to guard the Institute."

"Agreed," said Daladier. "Is R. Ishihara of equal importance?"

"No, he isn't," said Jane. "Dr. Nystrom is critically important. Ishihara is only important in that he is helping Wayne Nystrom."

"I do not expect them," Hunter added. "This is merely a contingency, in the event that you have the opportunity to act."

Steve should have taken his turn to change. Instead, looking unusually grim, he had not moved. Jane frowned at him, puzzled.

"Those who are ready, please enter the sphere," said Hunter. "I shall set the timer and the console controls."

"You don't need me," said Steve. "I'm not going."

Steve looked around at all of them, knowing he would get an argument.

"*What*?" Jane demanded angrily.

"I don't think I should go," said Steve.

"I am surprised," said Hunter, studying his face. "Is something wrong?"

"No, nothing's wrong. But I'm not necessary. I started thinking about this when I woke up this morning, but I didn't really decide until now."

"What are you talking about?" Jane glared at him. "Decide what?"

"You don't need me this time. Look, in the Late Cretaceous, maintaining our camp out in the wild was critical to survival. I made a real contribution. On the trip to Jamaica, well, I went because I had agreed to—you could have managed without me."

"Not after Rita took off on her own," said Jane.

"And last time, as I think back on the trip to Roman Germany, we spent most of our energy trying to find each other after we split up. I don't think I added anything."

"Not true," said Hunter. "You helped carry our belongings and accompanied Jane, allowing us to divide the team when it seemed advisable."

"Well, anyhow, you really don't need me in a more recent human era like 1941." Steve turned to Judy. "Aren't all the necessities for human life going to be available in Moscow at that time?"

"Well, generally. But it's in the middle of a war, where everyone has hardships—some of them severe." She shrugged. "It's hard to say exactly what life will be like for us on a given day."

"I can't help with that. Anything that's happened because of wartime conditions is beyond my help, anyway. And Hunter can protect everyone. He can also carry the duffel bag more easily than I can."

Jane looked at Hunter helplessly.

"It is true that your duties have changed with each mission," said Hunter. "However, your help has sometimes occurred in situations that were not predictable beforehand. You understand the challenges and the constraints under which the team works. I believe we still need your participation."

Steve shook his head. "I doubt it. You can keep Jane and Judy with you and concentrate on MC 4 and Wayne. I'd like to take my pay for the earlier trips and go on home."

"How can you just walk *away* like this?" Jane shouted. "We've all been working together. And you didn't say anything at breakfast this morning to me. Why didn't you *tell* me?"

"I was still thinking about it," said Steve, surprised at her vehemence.

"You're betraying all of us." She turned her back angrily and folded her arms.

"You hired me, remember? I didn't take any special oath of loyalty. It's a job. And you don't need me to do it." Steve turned to Hunter. "You remember when you came up to my place on the mountain?"

"Of course," said Hunter.

"You needed someone familiar with the outdoors to make and maintain camp for your team in the age of dinosaurs. That was your basis for hiring me."

"Yes, that is correct."

"You don't need that in Moscow in 1941. And you didn't really need it in Jamaica."

"We needed you in Port Royal!" Jane whirled around again, making her long coat swirl. "Don't you remember what we did together—sneaking up on pirate ships and getting into those sword fights? And jumping off to row ashore? What if I'd been *alone*, Steve?"

"You wouldn't have been in that situation without me to start with," said Steve. "I'm glad I helped. But you know every mission is different."

"Your skills could have been necessary in Germany of A.D. 9, as well," said Hunter. "The wilderness had many dangers. You did accompany Jane at important times. We did not utilize most of your skills, I admit, but we might have needed them."

"All right, granted," said Steve. "But not in Moscow. Not in the time you're going to visit now."

"You've been part of this team!" Jane insisted

angrily. "Your companionship and experience are part of this team, too. How can you do this?"

Steve just shook his head. "I don't like the idea of being tied down. Hunter, send someone up to my shack with my pay. Judy, nice to meet you. Good luck, Hunter. Bye, Jane." He turned toward the door.

"Where are you going now?" Hunter asked.

"Back home, of course."

"How will you get there?"

"That's my worry." Steve slipped out the door of the room. The door closed behind him and his footsteps sounded quickly down the hall.

Hunter watched Steve go, reviewing his past behavior quickly. Nothing Steve had said or done recently had revealed any desire to quit the team. He was as startled as Jane.

"What are we going to do?" Jane asked quietly.

"How important is he?" Judy asked. "As the newcomer, I don't really know what's going on."

"He is essentially correct," said Hunter. "The tasks for which I originally hired him are no longer necessary. We shall go." He hoisted the duffel bag and passed out some of the Soviet currency to Jane and Judy. "First I shall tend the console and then I shall help you both into the sphere."

Jane and Judy looked at each other in surprise. Hunter was aware that as humans, their emotions did not shift instantly. However, he saw no reason to delay their departure further.

In a moment, Hunter had set the timer in the console. After Jane and Judy were safely inside the big sphere with the duffel bag, he climbed inside and shut the door. As always, the interior was dark and crowded. Then the sphere vanished.

All three of them tumbled onto cold, hard ground in near darkness. The barest hint of sunset was still visible in the west. The sky was clear and the moon threw a gentle light. Their breath frosted in the icy air.

Hunter turned up his hearing and infrared vision to scan the immediate area for danger. They were in open, barren land a short distance from the edge of Moscow. No one was near them. "We are safe for the moment."

"Where are we?" Judy got to her feet, brushing off her coat. "My ears are cold already." She untied her scarf from her neck and moved it over her head, knotting it under her chin.

Jane imitated her.

"We are on the outskirts of Moscow," said Hunter. "I brought us here to avoid appearing right in front of the local people." He pointed. "The city is blacked out because of the war, but if you look that way, you can see some light leaking out of the shades of windows here and there."

"I see them," said Judy.

"Are you warm enough?" Hunter asked.

"Yeah. And walking will help," said Judy.

"I'm okay," said Jane. "But I wish Steve had come."

"The walk will not be as long as it looks," said Hunter. He shouldered the duffel bag and they started.

"Hunter, have you discussed the chaos theory of history with Judy?"

"Not yet," said Hunter.

"I'm familiar with it," said Judy, in a derisive tone. "But I just don't buy it. Not every little, tiny event is going to change the sweep of major historical trends."

"In our experience, that has proved to be true of the most insignificant events," said Hunter.

"I don't want to hear about any rigid rules," said Judy. "Now, obviously, we won't assassinate Stalin or Hitler; we probably couldn't do it if we tried. Anything less than that is not likely to change the course of World War II from where we stand."

"You sound like Steve on this subject," said Jane. "Except that you know your history."

"Only large-scale changes can alter the flow of history," said Judy. "I see nothing wrong with an aggressive involvement with events while we're here."

"I admit that the most extreme chaos theory of history has not been supported by our actions," said Hunter. "In our first three missions into the past, we clearly caused certain changes by our very presence and behavior, even though the changes were all very minor. No identifiable changes occurred in our own time."

"Exactly my point," said Judy.

"Our remaining problem is this," Hunter added. "None of us knows exactly when the threshold of change will be crossed. At some point, the sheer weight of the small changes may precipitate a major one. So we must remain very concerned about this principle."

"I just don't see how the three of us alone can bring about that much change," said Judy. "The threshold is pretty high, if you ask me."

"I shall point out an example pertaining to Egypt," said Hunter. "During the Napoleonic Wars, a battle was fought in Egypt between the British and French. The French defeat was significant but not ultimately decisive. However, a French soldier digging a trench unearthed the Rosetta stone, which led to the later translation of ancient Egyptian hieroglyphics. That translation in turn gave archaeologists the ability to read important writings, illuminating many centuries of history."

"Yeah, I know about that," said Judy.

"I didn't," said Jane. "What you're saying is that the chaotic result of the French campaign was extremely important in ways that had nothing to do with the war."

"Yes," said Hunter.

"We might argue that the Rosetta stone, or something similar, would have been found within a few decades anyway," said Judy. "Or that making these translations of hieroglyphics did not, after all, make a real difference in the development of society and industry in our own time at all."

"Isn't that an odd argument for a historian?" Jane asked. "To suggest that learning about history isn't important?"

"Wait a minute." Judy laughed. "I'm just saying that importance is relative."

"I submit the following," said Hunter. "Many young people who will enter positions of importance in the Cold War that follows World War II were present in the Battle of Moscow. Altering which of them live or die could change the course of the Cold War, theoretically bringing about the global nuclear war that was in fact just barely avoided during the second half of the twentieth century."

"Well, I can see that argument. But maybe the individuals wouldn't matter that much. Maybe the situation dictated decisions, not the individuals. Sometimes that happens."

"Our immediate concern is MC 4," said Jane.

"Yes," said Hunter. "I believe that when MC 4 returns to full size, the First Law will drive him to interfere with the war if he can."

Jane nodded. "With MC 4's background in ethics and morality, his interpretation of the First Law will probably have him focus on individuals who make decisions."

"Judy, where would that take him?" Hunter asked.

"You're saying he will attempt to interfere with those who give the orders and carry out the mass destruction," Judy said slowly. "That could take him almost anywhere. Immense suffering takes place on both sides, on all levels. These two regimes both operated on fear and power emanating from the top. Decisions to cooperate and obey orders had to be made all the way down the command structure to the bottom."

"Sounds horrible," said Jane.

"It was," said Judy. "Or, I should say, it *is*."

They walked in silence for a while. As they drew closer, Hunter observed the buildings of Moscow. Clearly, the city was not under attack tonight.

"We must find shelter for the night," he said. "Judy, where would this be most likely?"

"Well, let me think a minute. We're in the first week of December 1941. By this time, the German advance has been close to Moscow for several months. It has stalled right now, but Moscow has been bombarded. Many people have fled the city and others have been displaced by the destruction."

"Are you saying that shelter will be difficult to find?" Hunter asked.

"No. Actually, thousands of people are living in schools and empty warehouses. Soviet factories have been moved east across the Ural mountains to get them away from the Germans, so lots of big buildings are empty. We should be able to join a crowd of people in one of them. After all, it's only early evening. Everyone will still be awake."

"Good."

By the time the team had entered the city streets, Hunter could see that the city was still active in its relative darkness. Crowds of people were trudging home on the sidewalks from their daily responsibilities, a few laughing and talking but most quiet and exhausted. From behind all the drapes and shades in the windows, hints of light revealed that people were inside.

Jane wrinkled her nose. "What's the smell? Something's burning?"

"Coal," said Judy. "They burn it to heat buildings. The smoke always smells like that."

"Yuck."

Judy nudged Hunter and pointed down one block, where a big truck with an open back had stopped. A large group of people, mostly women, were climbing down and going into the entrance of a building. Hunter changed direction and led his companions down to the entrance.

Two dour men of average height but substantial girth stood by the doors in heavy overcoats and scarves, watching the crowd stream inside.

"We should pose as a family," said Judy quietly. "They will view us better that way."

"What do you suggest?"

"Given our looks, let's present you and Jane as brother and sister; I'll be a cousin. And you must have some reason for not being in the army."

"What reason will work?"

"Can you affect an exaggerated limp?"

"Yes, I understand." Hunter nodded and began to limp on his left leg. "This will fit perfectly with our possession of the military duffel bag. And it is time for us to switch to speaking Russian."

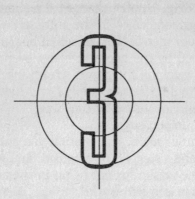

When the team reached the entrance to the darkened building, one of the men guarding it moved to block his way. "Yes, comrade? I have not seen you before."

"Our home is destroyed," said Hunter. "We need a place to stay." He hefted the duffel bag on the strap. "We have no other belongings now but this."

"Where was this home?" The other man glared suspiciously at him.

"To the west of Moscow," said Judy quickly. "On a collective farm. Overrun by the Germans, now."

Hunter could see that she had been caught off guard by the question. He did not respond, concerned that he might contradict something she would say. She still had the best chance of answering to the guard's satisfaction.

"The Germans have been in their positions for weeks. Where have you been until tonight?"

"A warehouse," said Judy. "It was too crowded. They threw us out."

"You are husband and wife?" The guard looked back and forth between them.

"No," said Hunter. He nodded toward Jane. "This is my sister."

"Yes," said Jane. "Our parents died in the war."

"I'm his cousin," Judy added.

"And where did your parents die?"

Jane hesitated. "I was so upset when it happened . . ." She turned to Judy uncomfortably.

"We were on the run," said Judy, with more confidence now. "They were killed somewhere along the highway from Minsk, near Smolensk."

"And where exactly was your collective farm?"

"Just south of Smolensk."

"What was it called?"

"The Smolensk Collective Number Two."

The guard studied her face for a moment, apparently without more questions.

"You sustained an injury, comrade," said the other man, more patiently. "What happened?"

"My cousin was wounded in the Battle of Leningrad," Judy said proudly. "He was nearly killed. When he could walk, they sent him home to take care of us."

"Welcome, comrade," said the second man. "Let them in, Yevgeny. We cannot have them freeze all night."

The first man nodded and stepped aside.

Hunter led his team inside. They found themselves in a very large, single room that took up the entire ground floor. Two stories high, with windows that had been painted black, it was already crowded. A few people had brought chairs or cots, but most were spreading blankets on the bare wooden floor to mark their personal territory.

"Looks like a warehouse," said Judy. "It probably housed industrial materials that were shipped east with the factory equipment."

"People are favoring the sides and the front," said Hunter. "The back corners are not taken yet. Let us move there quickly and take one for its relative privacy."

Hunter patiently picked his way through the crowded room to the right rear corner. It was far from the heating vents, but not too cold. He set down the duffel bag.

"Over there," said Judy, pointing across the room. "Look. An old woman is passing out blankets to some people."

"We should get some for the two of you," said Hunter.

"You stay here," said Judy. "Protect our space. I'll get them."

"Take Jane," said Hunter. "I shall watch you carefully from here."

"Oh, I don't think we're in immediate danger." Judy headed for the blankets and Jane followed her.

Hunter observed that his concern was overstated. Under stress, humans could be short-tempered and violent, but the people here had fallen into a regular routine, beaten down by the hardships of war and exhaustion. From what Judy had said, this society itself also regimented them severely.

Judy and Jane returned with some blankets.

"They're wool," Judy said, handing one to Hunter. "Scratchy, but clean and heavy."

"I'm not complaining," said Jane. "It's the only padding we'll have on the floor, too."

"Use mine for your padding as well." Hunter gave his back to Judy.

Judy and Jane spread out the blankets to sit on. Hunter sat down on the bare floor and leaned back against the cold wall. He saw that no one was close enough to overhear him if he spoke quietly.

"Judy, where would MC 4 go in order to prevent the most harm with the least effort?"

"Well . . ." Judy glanced around. Then she whispered, switching to English. "He might try to stop the NKVD—the Soviet secret police. They act paranoid, and are irrationally cruel to everyone. Their own people are their primary target. They are always hunting out potential security risks to the government, but that often means execution or lifetime imprisonment for people who merely ask for information or express an opinion. And for talking about them, English is even better than Russian. We can't chance being understood."

"Are they actually a greater danger than the upcoming battle itself?" Hunter shifted to English, leaning close to her and lowering his own voice to a whisper.

"The battle will cause a lot of suffering," said Judy. "But the Soviets will win the Battle of Moscow. It's their first major victory of the war."

"Are you sure it's safe to speak English?" Jane whispered, glancing around. "If we're heard, they'll know we aren't Russian peasants."

"For the NKVD, yes," said Judy. "We're better off raising suspicion than being overheard clearly."

"On this subject, then, we shall risk it," whispered Hunter. "However, Judy, the Soviets do not know they are going to win. MC 4 may or may not know; I cannot assume his motives or information in choosing to come here. Jane has surmised that he has come here because of his responsibility for ethics in Mojave Center, but we have no certainty. So my question about the danger from the NKVD still stands."

"All right," said Judy. "I'll give you the whole picture. Despite their impending counterattack, the Soviets are still on the defensive because this is their territory. As they see it, they must either surrender to Nazi cruelty or run. If they flee, they expect to suffer even more from the winter and the pursuing enemy than if they fight. The Russian people are caught between Stalin, Hitler, and the Russian winter. Those are unbelievably horrible options."

"You are saying what?" Hunter asked.

"I'm saying that the Russians don't feel they have much of a choice about whether to fight. So MC 4 can't go to Stalin, or the Soviet generals, and talk them out of the violence. And if he tries to persuade the NKVD to be more reasonable, they'll throw him in prison or blow his electronic brains out."

"The German army is the aggressor on the military front, then," said Jane. "Maybe he'll try to stop them."

"He doesn't really need to," said Judy. "Since the Soviets are going to drive them back anyhow. By this time, the German army is almost frozen in place."

"What happened to them?" Hunter asked. "How

could they get this far and then fail without being defeated?"

"They were handled with tremendous incompetence by Hitler. And one of the top German generals refused to issue winter clothing to his troops. He was afraid they would lose confidence in his personal guarantee that they would take shelter in Moscow before the winter turned cold."

"That's crazy," said Jane.

"That's right," said Judy grimly. "If it weren't for the suffering of all the ordinary people caught in the middle, I'd say these two regimes—Hitler's and Stalin's—simply deserved each other."

"Suppose MC 4 convinced the Germans to turn away from Moscow," said Hunter.

"I don't see how," said Judy. "Hitler's not at the front, and he makes the ultimate strategic decisions."

"Please consider the supposition."

"Well—if the battle doesn't take place, that would be a change of some magnitude," she said slowly. "But I can't see it reversing the course of the war. The Soviets will still have the initiative on this front."

"Perhaps the German command should not be our first priority," said Hunter. "I brought us here because the data in the sphere console told me that Moscow, not the German lines to the west, was MC 4's destination. The site of the nuclear explosion confirmed it."

"MC 4 may move quickly once he returns to full size," said Jane. "We don't know if he would choose to stay in Moscow or not."

"The center of the recent explosion in our own

time was in Moscow," Hunter added. "Of course, MC 4 could have moved around a great deal between now and our own time, once he had the advantages of normal human size. For now, we will remain in Moscow and try to learn if anyone of MC 4's description has been noticed."

Judy nodded.

"Do we have a plan of action?" Jane asked.

"I do not want to separate the team," said Hunter. "As you know, we have had reason to regret doing so in each of the previous missions."

"And without Steve, one of us would be alone," Jane added, shaking her head.

"Dinnertime," said Judy, nodding toward the front.

Much of the crowd had lined up to receive meager rations of bread, boiled potatoes, and water from the long table. The remainder were still arranging their personal belongings at various places around the floor. Only a few had already been served.

Hunter stood up. "We must join the line."

"Time to switch back to Russian," said Jane.

Hunter led them to the rear of the line, where they waited patiently. They passed through the line, receiving their dinner of thin soup and a hard roll in an odd assortment of dishes. Then they returned to their corner to eat.

Jane and Judy sat in the corner itself. Hunter placed himself where his body would block the view of them from the other occupants of the room. Then he slipped some of their dried meat out of the duffel bag for Jane and Judy to eat while no one else could see them.

Hunter observed that the Russians were still wide awake after dinner. His team's first two missions had taken place in summer and the most recent in early fall. This was the first one to take place in winter, with early nightfall. Bedtime would not arrive for a few hours yet. Of his team members, Jane had recently completed a full night's sleep, though Judy had risen very early to make the trip to Mojave Center.

As Jane finished her dinner, chewing on her hard roll, she saw Judy lean to her right to see past Hunter.

"You know," Judy said quietly. "After years of studying this era, I finally have a chance to see the people of this time for myself. Since most of the people here are women, I'm sure that I can approach them comfortably for a little conversation."

"Please be careful," said Hunter.

"I'll return our dishes when we're all finished," said Judy. "Then I'll see if I can strike up a conversation on my way back through the crowd. Maybe I can learn something."

"You want to talk to people?" Jane asked, glancing at Hunter.

"*Please* be very careful," Hunter repeated.

Judy smiled. "Don't worry. I have as much fear of the NKVD as anyone here."

"We do not want to change anyone's behavior unnecessarily," Hunter added.

"I don't think anything I can say here will change the outcome of the battle."

"I'll go with you," said Jane.

They collected their empty dishes and worked their way back to the front of the warehouse. Jane knew that Judy believed Hunter had an exaggerated fear of how much influence any of the team could possibly have on historical events. So Jane wanted to keep tabs on how Judy handled herself.

Judy took her time on the return trip, looking around for someone to approach. Many people were obviously as comfortable as they could get, having grown accustomed to life in these conditions. Others tended babies or small children and were too occupied to make small talk. Jane followed her, also surveying the crowd.

"How about her?" Jane asked quietly, pointing to one side of the room.

A tired, bent, elderly woman fumbled with her blanket, trying to shake it out with stiff, gnarled fingers. She shuffled to one side, still stooped over, and shook it again. No one paid any attention to her.

Judy worked her way toward her in the crowd. The old woman was obviously alone, though others sat nearby with their own families. By the time Judy reached her, the old woman was on her hands and knees, patiently smoothing and straightening the blanket on the hard floor.

Judy squatted down and tugged the wrinkles out of the last corner. The old woman looked up at her, startled. She looked scared.

"I'm only helping," Judy said gently. "I'm sorry if I surprised you."

The old woman nodded, still watching Judy cautiously. Then she glanced up at Jane, who had come to stand behind Judy. The woman's face was sharp-featured and deeply lined. After a moment, she relaxed a little and sat down on the blanket.

"I'm Judy Taub. What's your name?"

"Ivana Voronov," she said quietly. She smiled, though, for the first time. "Please sit down." She patted the blanket and looked up at Jane again. "And your friend, too."

Judy squatted down on the blanket, keeping her boots off of it. Jane joined her. The old woman looked back and forth between them, waiting for someone to say something.

"We're new in this shelter," said Judy.

"Oh? Where have you been?"

"Well . . . on the move. We've been displaced by the war." Judy shrugged. "We saw everyone getting off the buses. Where were you? In a work brigade?"

"Oh, yes. We're digging the big ditches to the west."

"Ditches?" Jane asked, turning to Judy.

"Antitank ditches," said Judy quietly. "A quarter million Muscovites are digging them with hand shovels. Three-quarters of the workers are women, since the men are either in the army or working in heavy industry. The ditches are to block the advance of German tanks from the west of the city."

"By hand?" Jane shook her head, impressed. "Hard work. Especially in this weather."

Ivana grimaced, rubbing her hands. "I can't do very much at my age. My hands hurt all the time. So does my back. These young girls, now, they work very hard."

"Thousands of people abandoned their jobs and homes during the past few months to get away from Moscow," said Judy. "Fleeing the Germans long before the battle. Ivana, why didn't you go then?"

"Yes, yes, those with money or companions or relatives to see all hurried away to the east. I had no means to travel and nowhere to go."

"What about your family?" Judy asked gently. "Do you have family members in the army?"

"My sons are in the Red Army," she said quietly, lowering her gaze to the blanket. "I have heard nothing from them for over a year."

"Where's your husband?" Jane asked.

"He was taken." Ivana's voice was almost a whisper. She lowered her head, hiding her face.

"You don't mean by the Germans, do you?" Judy whispered slowly.

Ivana shook her head, wiping away tears.

Even Jane understood that the NKVD had taken her husband.

Judy leaned closer to her, still whispering. "Do you know why?"

"No. It was two years ago, when so many were taken. They gave no reason and I have heard nothing."

Judy nodded.

Jane glanced at the people around them. If they were listening, they were pretending otherwise. However, Ivana had become a liability to them. With her husband arrested, she herself might be under the watch of the secret police. Her neighbors would not befriend her for fear that they, too, would come under the scrutiny of the NKVD.

"Have you been in this work brigade long?" Jane asked. "Staying here?"

"Oh, yes." Ivana nodded, apparently glad to change the subject. "I've been in it for a couple of months. My own building was destroyed by shelling, so I had to come here. But it's not a bad place. The shelter is good and they always have food here."

"Do you know most of the people? At least by sight?" Jane leaned closer, too.

"I suppose. I don't talk to very many people." She shrugged, embarrassed.

"How about the other work brigades? Do you work alongside others?"

"Sometimes, yes. Not always. Our location each day is different. So long as we dig the ditches, no one cares which brigade we are next to or where we dug the day before."

Jane turned to Judy. "I want to get Hunter. She might be able to help us locate . . . our friend."

"All right," said Judy. "Good idea. I'll stay here with Ivana."

Jane stood up and patiently worked her way over to Hunter. Now that the crowd had finished dinner and had taken their positions for the night, with some of them stretched out to relax, the way was more difficult. It took her a minute or a little more to reach him. He protectively watched her progress.

"Come and meet someone," she said quickly. "I think she can help us." She turned to point to Judy and Ivana.

They were gone.

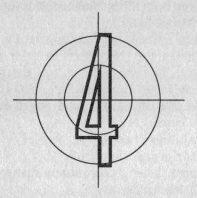

Hunter looked where Jane pointed. He saw the empty blanket neatly arranged on the floor. Then he scanned the room quickly for Judy and saw her by the door.

Two men in long, black wool overcoats were escorting Jane and an elderly woman out the front door of the warehouse. In the front, where others could see them, the crowd in the warehouse had fallen silent. Yet they also looked away, at each other or at their belongings, pretending not to notice as they kept their hands busy with little tasks.

"Who are they?" Jane whispered.

"Perhaps they are NKVD agents," Hunter whispered back. "I would guess that they must be."

"Oh, no." Jane clutched his arm. "I'm sure they are. Ivana's husband—that's the old woman's name—was taken by them a couple of years ago."

"I have to get Judy back," said Hunter, feeling a surge of tension from the First Law. "You will be much safer here than chasing the NKVD with me. Do you agree?"

"Yes. I'm sure I'll be fine right here. I'll stay here in the crowd and lie low. And I have my lapel pin to call you if I need to."

"Good." Hunter had no doubt that he could trust Jane's judgment; unlike Steve, she had never caused trouble by improvising her moves. "In this crowd, of course, you will be in danger of being overheard if I call you, so I cannot."

Jane nodded. "Get going."

Hunter did not want to be seen leaving the warehouse. While Judy and Jane had returned the dishes and had spoken to Ivana, he had studied the layout of the building itself. Moving casually with his overcoat bundled under one arm, he worked his way to the rest room and went inside.

As he had surmised, its outside wall had one long, vertical window in a wooden casement. He turned on the water in the sink to create noise and pulled the window open with a creak and a low rumble. Then he turned off the water, slipped outside, and slowly pulled the window down again. It made more noise, but now he knew it would not be too loud. Once it was closed, he shook out his overcoat and put it on.

In the cold, clear winter night, Hunter turned and jogged toward the front of the warehouse.

Judy was scared as the men took her and Ivana out the front door. They were not rough, but held their prisoners' arms firmly. Outside, they pushed Judy forward against a large, black car without a word and frisked her.

She and Ivana were put into the back of the car. The men had not spoken at all. They got in, slammed the doors, started the engine, and pulled away from the warehouse.

Ivana was quivering in terror, speechless and beyond tears. Judy reached over and held her hand. Ivana did not seem to notice.

Judy's studies had taught her that Stalin was responsible for the deaths of more people than any other individual in history. She knew about the labor camps in the Gulag where people were tortured, starved, and worked to death, and about the mass murders committed by his agents here at the front. These people were beyond rational argument.

Truth and accuracy were not valued by this government. Just a few months before this time, the NKVD had threatened to arrest Red Air Force pilots as "panic mongers" when they had honestly reported the German advance toward Moscow. The values of the NKVD were so unpredictable that dealing with them was extremely dangerous.

Judy did not dare speak. Remembering her lapel communicator, however, she reached up and switched it on. The agents had not bothered with a thorough search yet; they might take it from her later. Now, however, Hunter might pick up some sounds through it, such as the engine noise from the car. She knew that the agents had ignored the modest pin as a danger because, in this time, no radio transmitter could be made that small.

The agents had come for Ivana without explanation. Apparently they had taken Judy because she had been with Ivana. That was all Judy knew about them.

She looked out the car window into the darkened city. Searchlights swept the cold, clear sky for enemy planes, but no attack was occurring. Even artillery shells were not falling. She knew that at this time, the German army was virtually immobile with the cold and was running out of both supplies and human energy as winter deepened.

Even with her knowledge of this period, she could not recall exactly when the aerial attacks took place, and when they had been discontinued. Tonight, apparently, Moscow was spared. Hoping that the ride would last a long time, she wondered if the lapel pin was actually transmitting.

When Hunter came around the corner of the warehouse, he found the streets deserted. He saw a single car driving away from the front of the warehouse. He stopped and shifted to his infrared vision, which made visible the silhouettes of Judy and Ivana in the backseat.

Hunter watched for a moment, unsure of what to do. Though he had more physical stamina than a human, even he could not keep up with a car for long, so when it was out of sight and hearing he would lose it.

Suddenly Hunter began to receive the static and engine noise from Judy's transmitter. He understood that she had switched on her lapel pin. Now he had a chance to follow the car even after it left the range of his aural and visual sensors.

Before following the car, however, he decided to make himself less conspicuous by altering his appearance. His height was his most obvious feature, so he reduced it to six feet. Naturally, he could not change his total mass, so he remained just as heavy, but he now possessed a very solid, stocky build. He made his face broader to remain consistent with his new body. However, because he wanted Judy to be able to recognize him, he did not change his face very much. On their second mission he had done this, and when Jane had thought he was a buccaneer, she had clubbed him over the head with a belaying pin.

His clothes were now a problem. The bulky overcoat and shirt were still adequate, but his thicker waist threatened to pop the buttons on the waistband of his pants. He slimmed his waist again slightly, putting more mass into his legs. Then he paused to fold under his sleeves and cuffs, since they were now too long for his shorter limbs.

The red taillights of the car were nearly out of sight by now. Hunter could still hear the engine noise through Judy's transmitter, however. He took off at a run.

The car turned a corner to the right and vanished. Hunter maintained his pace at first. Then, when he heard another vehicle coming up the street behind him, he ducked into the shadow of a doorway.

He lost more time as he waited, but he could not afford to be stopped by military police, or more NKVD agents, or anyone else in authority. At least the streets had very few people out who would notice him or report him. When the way was clear again, he ran as fast as he could, and soon made the same turn himself.

Ahead of him, the red taillights were already vanishing over a slight rise in the street. The black car had now joined a couple of other vehicles going in the same direction. However, with the radio signal to follow, Hunter could still identify the one he followed.

No pedestrians were on this street, either. Though the city was very dark, the clear sky gave Hunter enough moonlight to maneuver. He could hear the radio signal from Judy slowly and inexorably fading as the car drove away from him. Now he hoped that they would stop or at least be delayed before he lost the signal entirely.

Jane sat huddled in her corner of the warehouse, feeling very much alone. No one bothered her and, from what she could see, no one even seemed to have noticed her. She reassured herself with the reminder that, of course, Hunter would come hurrying back if she called him. On the other hand, she would not interfere with his hunt for Judy without an absolutely critical emergency right here. She was uncomfortable simply because she felt so isolated here in this cold, gloomy place.

If Steve had come on this mission, he would be here with her, right now.

Judy stiffened when the car pulled into the rear lot of a large building. The two men opened the back doors and pulled Judy and Ivana out by their arms. As before, the men did not speak.

The inside of the building was dimly lighted, cold, and silent. In the shadows, Judy saw old, decorative wooden molding that had been ignored for years, judging by the filth collected around it.

From the regular distance separating the doors, she guessed it might have been a hotel in the Czarist years.

The footsteps of all four of them tapped loudly as they walked down a large hall. Judy and Ivana were taken to a small room lighted by a hanging lamp with a single bulb. Their escorts then left, loudly snapping the door lock into place. The room had no other doors and no windows.

Ivana quivered with fear. Judy looked around. The room was set up as an interrogation or meeting room, not as a prison cell. A long table ran down the center, with chairs on both sides of it. She eased Ivana into a chair, then pulled out another for herself, wondering how long they would have to wait for something else to happen.

"Ivana? Why would they want you?" Judy asked quietly. "Do you know?"

The old woman just stared at her.

"Why did they take your husband? What exactly happened? Maybe I can help somehow."

Ivana just shook her head. Then she looked up at the light fixture and around the nearly empty room. She gestured vaguely at the walls.

Finally Judy understood what Ivana was trying to express. Ivana was afraid that the room was bugged with secret listening devices. In this era, such devices would be very unsophisticated by the standards of Judy's time, but they would work. Judy simply nodded and stopped asking questions.

Suddenly Judy realized that if Hunter had been able to track her radio signal, it might also influence the NKVD reception. She decided, however, not to turn off her lapel pin. It was her only hope of telling Hunter where she was, so she would have to take the chance.

Now that the engine noise from the car was gone, she realized she should send a sound of some kind. She reached up and idly began tapping her lapel pin with her fingernails. Ivana paid no particular attention.

Judy decided that the fact that Ivana's husband had been taken was enough reason for Ivana to be arrested, too. If he was still alive somewhere, he might have done or said something that had brought this about. Her sons, wherever they were with the Red Army, might also have attracted the attention of the political commissars assigned to the military.

Judy remembered one case from the Stalin era in which a man was sent to prison for thirty-five years because he asked an NKVD agent why his neighbor had been arrested. For that matter, Judy's presence with Ivana in the crowded warehouse was the only reason that she had been taken.

Judy wondered why no one had questioned them yet.

As Hunter continued to run at a steady pace, except when he ducked out of sight from other vehicles, he realized that the signal from Judy was growing stronger. First the engine noise stopped, then he heard car doors opening and closing. Those sounds were followed by the creak of a building door and the sound of four sets of footsteps on an interior floor.

He knew that Judy and Ivana were unharmed so

far from the questions Judy had asked Ivana. From those he had also surmised that they were alone. Though conversation had stopped, the clear tapping and scratching sounds became louder with each stride he took.

Finally the radio signal was so strong that Hunter knew Judy was within a hundred meters of him. Some quick zigzags in his route helped him focus on the source of the transmission. She was inside a very large building right in front of him. Almost an hour had passed since he had left the warehouse.

The building was constructed of stone and brick. Most of its windows were completely dark, but the light shone around the shades on the first floor. Since the city was blacked out for the night, the external lights were off.

Hunter assessed his internal energy level. The prolonged run in cold weather had lowered his reserves significantly, but he would be able to function normally for a while yet. He could not estimate how long, because the length of time would depend on his energy expenditure in rescuing Judy and the duration he spent in the cold. Certainly the First Law gave him no choice about attempting to help Judy immediately.

Before planning his actions, he considered the complex of First Law imperatives weighing on him. Most importantly, he could not interfere with the NKVD's historical actions. He could not knowingly create any changes in the course of history. Of almost equal importance, he had to protect Judy from harm. As he had discussed with his team in the briefing before this mission, however, he now understood that the historical process would clearly accept some small level of involvement from him.

Three approaches seemed open to him. The first, direct confrontation, risked violence against Judy and precipitating a change of actions by the NKVD toward Ivana, so he discarded that. The second was stealth, but he worried that sneaking into the building would take too long, since the NKVD might act quickly against its two new prisoners. That left a simple bluff as the most direct and least violent course of action.

As Steve had sometimes reminded him, improvising could be very useful. Hunter prepared himself to try it as he walked up to the front entrance, assuming a casual, confident walk. The front door was locked, but he heard the metal pins rattle inside the knob. They sounded simple and primitive. In all likelihood, they would break easily.

He grasped the knob and forced it to turn. The insides of the lock snapped and ground as he broke them. However, a second lock held a metal bolt in place and he had no way to grab hold of it.

Hunter fingered the doorjamb. The wood was old and fairly solid, but it could be broken. Doing so would make noise and attract attention inside the building. He decided that he would have to take that risk.

Bracing himself with his legs, he crouched and positioned himself to spring forward. Then he slammed his entire weight against the door at the point where it would apply the most force against the bolt. The bolt tore through the wooden doorjamb with a splintering sound as the door opened.

Then he walked inside and calmly closed the door behind him.

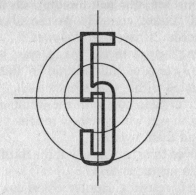

At this late hour, no one sat behind the front counter. The lobby was dark, though a light was on in a main hallway. A burly man in a plain gray business suit was bending over a coffee percolator on a small wooden table about halfway down the hall. He looked up in surprise and then walked forward, frowning.

"Who are you, comrade? This office is closed. What do you want here?"

At the sound of his voice, another door opened and two more men, dressed in similar suits, followed the first man toward Hunter.

"Where are the new prisoners?" Hunter demanded. "I must see them immediately."

"Are you with the agency?" The first man spoke more cautiously. "We have not met. My name is—"

Hunter pushed past him. "Stop interfering! I shall have you all on report! Where are they?" The radio signal was very strong, telling him that Judy was in a room right down the hall in front of him.

"We must see your identification," another man protested. "Please, comrade. We can all cooperate after procedures have been followed."

Hunter glared into the man's eyes, gambling that the system of intimidation in this society also operated within this agency itself. "I cannot be bothered right now with the whining of subordinates. If you will not show me the prisoners, I shall find them myself!"

He shoved this man, also, but the third reached up to grab his upper arm.

Instead of resisting, Hunter looked down at this man's face, as well. "I hear the weather is very cold out at the front. Since you have so much energy, they could use you there. Or perhaps you would prefer an assignment to Vladivostok, where the Siberian wind will keep you safe from German tanks."

Suddenly uncertain, the other man stepped back, glancing at his two companions, and released Hunter.

Carrying the bluff forward, Hunter strode past the third man and moved toward the room from which the radio signal came.

Earlier that night, Dr. Wayne Nystrom had landed with a thump on hard ground. He looked at his companion, the humaniform robot R. Ishihara. They seemed to have arrived in their new time and place safely.

"You okay, Ishihara?"

"Yes," the robot said calmly.

Wayne surveyed the dry, frozen rolling plains around them. The sky was clear but the sun was red in the west, low over the horizon. "Well, it looks right so far. If I calculated correctly, we're on the Russian steppe just to the rear of the German lines west of Moscow in December of 1941. It looks like the steppe in December, I think, but I don't see anyone. Good for us that there's no snow."

"I hear the sounds of primitive machinery faintly in the distance," said Ishihara. "To the east of us. I expect we have arrived where you intended."

"What kind of machines?"

"Rough internal combustion engines, I believe. A few small vehicles. I hear nothing to suggest that large-scale movement or violence is occurring at this moment."

"Good." Wayne tugged his long fur cloak tighter around the knee-length tunic he wore. "The only trouble with coming directly here from Germany in A.D. 9 is that we're still wearing these clothes."

"We shall be warm, at least," Ishihara observed. He was dressed similarly. "Unless we find shelter, that is very important."

"Yeah. I'm sure we can get contemporary clothes from someone, somehow. I wonder what the Germans of this time will make of us when they see us." Wayne grinned wryly. "They certainly won't believe that we just arrived after visiting their distant ancestors."

"No." Ishihara looked at the weak sun, low in the sky to the west. "Night is falling. Even colder temperatures are imminent. I suggest we start walking."

"All right. Where to?"

"Well, I have begun monitoring the German

radio traffic. It is heavy, coming from the east of us in the same area as the machine sounds."

"You can understand German?"

"Yes. And I remind you that we dare not speak English in front of them, since the British and Americans are enemies of the Germans. Do you speak any Russian or German?"

"No Russian," said Wayne. "I studied German, but only to read technical research. I never spoke it much. What about you?"

"As a researcher at the Bohung Institute, I took all the necessary data for modern German and Russian a long time ago in order to read technical documents; also Japanese. So I shall be able to communicate here in those languages, though they will have evolved some in the forms I know."

"I still have my radio pin, but for now I'll let you handle this," said Wayne. "In fact, I have an extra; I kept the one I took from Steve in Germany. Anyhow, just lead the way to the closest people you can find."

Ishihara began to walk. Wayne fell into step with him. The open ground was uneven and hard and the wind whipped across them from the northwest. Nothing was visible across the barren, flat farmland.

"What is our long-range plan?" Ishihara asked. "Where do we expect to find that MC 4 has returned to his full size?"

"Well, I'm trying something a little different this time," said Wayne. "Actually, from the information I was able to obtain from the console on the sphere, I expect his miniaturization will end in Moscow, behind the Soviet lines."

"You do? Why did you bring us here, behind the German lines, then?"

"I've come after three of the component robots now, and every time, they have been adept at avoiding Hunter and his team when they first return to full size. He has been able to run them down eventually, but never right away."

"Do you expect MC 4 to come here somehow?"

"Yes. I have been considering the effect of the First Law on MC 4 when he analyzes the situation he has entered here. With a war going on, he will want to stop the violence by interfering with the aggressor."

"That would be the Germans, I believe."

"Exactly," said Wayne. "Since the German army has invaded Russian soil, I think he will come to the German lines to stop them if he can. If we're waiting for him, that will give us a jump on Hunter's team."

"How extensive is your knowledge of history at this time?" Ishihara asked.

"Very limited. I remember which countries fought on which side. And I know the Germans mistreated the Jews in Europe. Nazi Germany and the Soviet Union were pretty unpleasant, I guess."

"My data is not extensive, either," said Ishihara. "I merely have some summaries of the war given as part of my general education. But your evaluation of German treatment of Jews is an understatement of great magnitude."

"It is? Why, what—"

"Alert," Ishihara interrupted, suddenly looking into the distance to the east.

"You hear something?"

"I have picked up a radio transmission between a patrol vehicle and its base. The vehicle is on routine patrol, but it is coming this way."

"Have they seen us?"

"No, but they will soon, even in the waning light. I suggest that we devise a personal history we can give to them."

By now, even Wayne could hear the loud, rough engine in the distance. A tiny speck of headlights was barely visible in the dusk. Wayne and Ishihara kept walking.

"We'd better make it quick," said Wayne. "What do you suggest?"

"We must pretend to come from other countries. I have a Japanese name but not a Japanese appearance; I was merely named after a Japanese roboticist when I was created. Unlike Hunter, I do not have the ability to change my appearance. But maybe I can think of a way to trade on the German alliance with Japan somehow."

"What do you mean?" Wayne was watching the German patrol. So far, they apparently had not seen the two travelers yet, since the patrol was moving obliquely to them.

"I am not certain yet. I only know that my German, coming from many years in the future, will not pass as native to this time, so I won't try to fool anyone. However, your surname, 'Nystrom,' is Swedish. I see no reason to falsify it; your appearance matches that of your ancestors and Sweden was neutral in this war, though the other Scandinavian countries fought against Germany. We shall present you as Swedish."

"All right."

They walked in silence for a while. The headlights grew larger, bouncing over the hard soil. Finally the lights changed direction and began to move straight toward them.

"We have been seen," said Ishihara. "The patrol has just reported to their base that they are going to interrogate two men on foot. Apparently they had just enough sunlight left to see our movement."

Wayne grinned wryly. "I can hardly wait."

The small spot in the distance grew quickly as it raced toward them. Soon Wayne could see that it was a vehicle designed with a cab in the front and a large, open back full of soldiers. In the poor light, their gray uniforms and helmets made them almost invisible. They held rifles warily and two of them were tending some larger weapon mounted on a swivel.

"Do you know what that's called?" Wayne asked. "Their vehicle?"

"It might fit the term, 'armored car,'" said Ishihara. "My data lacks a diagram, however. That weapon on the front is a machine gun. The patrol is accustomed to violence. We must not risk angering them."

"Let's stop walking and wait."

Ishihara suddenly loosened his belt and reached into his tunic. "I believe we may be searched."

"We don't have any weapons."

"I suggest you give me the device that triggers the time travel sphere," said Ishihara. "I have opened a panel in my abdomen. I believe I can slip the device inside my torso safely."

"Well . . . okay." Wayne gave it to him. "But it doesn't look like a weapon. Why would they want it?"

"They will find it mysterious and might take it to study. Certainly we cannot afford to lose it."

"No—no argument about that."

The German patrol slowed carefully as it drew near. The soldiers looked over Wayne and Ishihara, their faces clearly puzzled by the long cloaks, tunics, and leggings. Some of them grinned as they muttered to each other.

One of the Germans spoke. Wayne could not understand him at all; certainly the archaic German he had learned for the previous mission was no help. Ishihara answered him politely, however. They spoke for a moment, then the German nodded. He gestured for two soldiers to jump down. They did so, their calf-length black boots thumping on the hard ground.

Ishihara leaned very close to Wayne and whispered in English. "They will frisk us. Cooperate with them. Their commander, a Korporal, has agreed to take us to German lines."

"Does he believe you? About my being Swedish and—whatever else you told him?"

"He has accepted it tentatively, but he is suspicious. I told him that I lived in Japan and took the name of a friend. We must remain very careful."

"Got it." Wayne, at the gesture of the German soldiers, raised his arms high over his head. He did not move as one of them quickly patted his clothing up and down the length of his body. Another did the same to Ishihara. Then both soldiers stepped back and pointed to the back of the armored car.

The soldiers helped Wayne and Ishihara mount the back of the armored car. The car lurched forward suddenly, into a wide turn. As it rumbled over the frozen ground, the soldiers ducked down behind the steel sides of the car to avoid the sharp wind. Wayne and Ishihara crouched with them. Around them, the nearest soldiers tugged on their fur cloaks and spoke quietly among themselves.

Hunter strode down the hall with the three NKVD agents protesting and pleading, but no longer trying to grab him. He could see that they remained intimidated by his threats and self-assuredness. They were still arguing with him as he reached the door to the room from which the radio signal emanated.

Ignoring the arguments of the agents, Hunter tried the doorknob and found the door locked. He turned and glared at the nearest man. "Open this door, comrade. Now."

"I have no key." He backed away.

"I do not believe you. You all have keys." Hunter turned to another man. "Open it. I insist."

The second man folded his arms and shook his head. "We must follow procedure, comrade. Surely you would not argue with us about that."

Hunter looked at the third man, who merely stared angrily back at him.

"Is that you, Hunter?" Judy's voice whispered to him through his internal receiver. "It's Judy—we're in here!"

Hunter decided that he could not wrestle with

all three agents to get a key, since he was hampered by the First Law requirement not to hurt them. Even with his greater strength, their sheer weight would stop him. On the other hand, he could not afford to leave Judy now.

A quick look into the crack between the door and the frame showed Hunter that this door did not have a bolt lock. He grasped the doorknob firmly, as he had done at the front door, and simply turned it slowly, with great force. Again, he heard the metal pins breaking. Then he shoved the door open and stepped inside the room.

Behind him, one agent gasped in surprise; another muttered to himself.

Hunter saw Judy rising from a chair on one side of a table. Gently, he took Ivana's arm and drew her to her feet; she would not look up at him. He walked her back to the doorway, while the agents stared at him in astonishment. This time they backed away, making room for her.

When Hunter had moved Ivana out of the room, he closed the door behind her, though of course the broken latch would not catch. A quick glance around the room showed him that it had no other exits. He had no way even to pretend that they were escaping through a window, another door, or even a large vent.

Judy watched him uncertainly. Hunter had already decided to take the greatest risk of exposing new technology he had ever considered on these missions. Before the agents regained their composure and entered, he walked over to Judy and triggered his belt control, taking them back to their own time.

Steve angrily marched down the hall away from Room F-12 in the Bohung Institute. He was mad at Jane for arguing with him. Even more, he was mad at himself for handling his resignation so poorly.

As he furiously replayed the conversation in his mind, he realized that he should have raised the subject earlier. Jane had a legitimate point about that. He could have shared his thoughts over breakfast, while he was still undecided.

At the same time, the episode reminded him that he really did not belong with educated, sophisticated company. Jane and Hunter would have handled themselves properly. So would all the historians who had joined them for one mission or another. He was better off up in his mountain shack.

Steve also pictured Jane in his mind. He had grown to like her a lot and, in Jamaica, he had felt they were growing closer. Then in Germany, they had not spent much time alone together. After all, those missions were serious, not a time to socialize. In any case, he still saw no reason that

a woman with her education would be interested
in a desert rat like himself. He was better off just
going home.

Steve turned the last corner into the main lobby and headed for the front doors. Then running
footsteps behind him got his attention. Puzzled,
he stopped and turned around.

"Steve!" Hunter's voice boomed from down the
hall. When he came bounding around the corner,
his long black overcoat flapping around him, he
was recognizable, but much altered—shorter and
broader than usual. "We need help."

"Huh? Come on, Hunter. We already settled
that. You don't need me."

"I have an emergency, Steve. We already left."
Hunter walked up to Steve, calmly now.

"You already left—and came back again?"

"Prematurely, I assure you. We have not even
begun to locate MC 4."

"What happened? You would never even consider coming back here like this in the middle of the
other missions."

"The First Law gave me no other choice. I had
to bring Judy back here to escape the potential of
extreme harm. Jane is in 1941 alone. Please help."

"Well, you can rejoin Jane right after you left
her, can't you? You can take care of her."

"I have considered this. The society we entered
is more complex than that of the Roman frontier
or the Jamaican buccaneers. The Stalin regime is
very dangerous and unpredictable. Finding MC 4
near the front of a major war will be more difficult
in the industrial age than in earlier times. I am
desperate for your help."

"You sure?" Steve looked at him skeptically.

"I even took another step out of desperation. In prior missions, I would not knowingly allow any local to see the team appear or vanish in time, because it might set up lines of thinking or behavior that have a significant effect on them. However, I had to escape with Judy from a confined room. NKVD agents saw us go in and will find us gone, even though the room has no exit except the one they are watching."

"Really? That's a big change for you." Steve suddenly realized how serious this was. "You must have been desperate."

"I have just taken two risks I would not have considered before. The irrationality and viciousness of the NKVD required me to take this lesser risk, rather than allow them the chance to torture Judy for information."

"Yeah," said Steve. "If they questioned her under torture, and she broke, they would learn that people were coming back from the future."

"These were among my considerations, yes."

"Well, I approve of your looser interpretation of chaos theory. But if any of you had changed history, it would be different right now, already."

"It could be changed, right now, in ways that we have not noticed in the few seconds since I have returned. Judy and I must go back. Please join us."

Steve sighed, but nodded. As much as he did not want to rejoin the team, he did like feeling needed. "I have one request, though, Hunter."

"What is that?"

"Would you change your appearance back to

normal, at least until this masquerade becomes necessary again? I can't get used to this."

"Oh, yes. Of course."

Steve walked with him quickly back to Room F-12.

In the room, Judy was pacing anxiously. "Are we ready? Can we go right back?"

"One more moment," said Hunter. He altered the shape of one forefinger slightly and plugged it into an electrical outlet. "I used an usually large amount of my stored energy during the night. Recharging from here will be very brief. Steve will come with us this time."

"Ivana can't survive the NKVD," said Judy frantically. "We have to help her somehow. Let's go right back."

"No," Hunter said firmly. "The NKVD took you because you happened to be with her. It was the result of our presence and I could justify taking you away again. However, the NKVD came for Ivana for reasons of their own. We did not precipitate her arrest in any way."

"You mean you *refuse* to help her?" Judy's eyes were wide with shock.

"I must. The First Law imperative to avoid changing history requires it."

"Hunter," she wailed. "Please. How can one elderly woman's freedom change the course of history? *How*? Tell me that, will you?"

"The potential chain of events we could set in motion would be impossible to predict."

"Maybe it won't make any difference. If you can't predict it, you can't know."

"The chance of harm to all the humans in the

time line is too great to risk," Hunter said patiently.

"All right. All right." Judy took a deep breath. "Just indulge me for a moment, though."

"How?"

"Give me an example of how saving Ivana might ruin history as we know it. She's already old, Hunter. And she probably won't survive long after this battle anyway, but her suffering could be eased."

"Ivana alone is not the problem. We must also consider the NKVD agents with whom she is in contact. The agents are younger and may survive into the Cold War era at the end of World War II, less than four years from her time. Their actions and opinions may be influenced by what happens to her—"

"Specifically, Hunter? What could these agents do that would matter?"

"Perhaps these agents will be politically active when the Soviet Union comes to an end in the early 1990s," said Hunter. "What if seeing the cruelty of their system to a helpless old woman in 1941 helped to change their opinion of the system they served? If we rescue Ivana somehow, maybe they will have one less doubt about their country."

"That's a very small change."

"I hate to argue his side," said Steve. "But in this case, I agree. These agents may have relatives who will remember family stories about this time, too, and be influenced."

"Ivana has two sons in the Red Army," Judy said slowly.

"They may die in the war or they may live into the Cold War years, too," said Hunter. "What if the fate of their mother spurred them to participate in the later dismantling of the Soviet Union? If she is rescued, they might—"

"Might not turn against the system," Judy finished for him. She sighed. "I get it. I guess I always did. I just wanted to hear you convince me."

"I am already worried that vanishing with you out of the room the way we did may have disturbed the NKVD agents significantly," said Hunter.

Judy nodded solemnly.

"Judy, did the agents photograph you?"

"Uh, no. They just put us in the room and made us wait. Maybe they were working out what questions to ask or something."

"You are still in danger of being recognized by the two agents who took you. We shall have to be especially careful to avoid them."

"Yes, I see."

"What's my identity this time?" Steve asked. "I can't be a slave, as I was in Roman times. But you still have to account for my not being Russian."

"Judy, do you have a suggestion?" Hunter asked.

"You can be a Turk from Central Asia," said Judy. "Or a Tatar, of old Mongol descent. Both were in the Soviet Union at that time."

"I took the sleep course for Russian, but not Mongol or any kind of Turkish," said Steve.

"In Moscow, Russian will be sufficient," said Judy. "Hunter, are we ready?"

"Yes. We shall go back to Moscow the following day, well after sunup, to look for Jane."

"What if something happened to her during the night?" Steve asked.

"I want to avoid returning Judy during that same night," said Hunter. "If something has happened to Jane, we shall return here and then go back earlier to find her if necessary. For now, we shall return after people have begun their daily routine, so that we can get lost in the crowd. Now that I have returned to my original appearance, the NKVD will not recognize me." He turned to Judy. "Perhaps we should wait while you get some sleep. You will lose a night's sleep with my plan."

"I'm too upset to sleep now," said Judy. "I want to go right back."

"Let's go," said Steve.

Early the next morning, Jane woke alone in the corner after a nervous, fitful sleep. She got in line with her companions for breakfast and then returned to her corner to eat a thin, tasteless gruel. After returning her bowl and spoon, she queued up for the rest room.

Jane finally took her turn and moved into a stall. She flushed the toilet to cover her voice somewhat from her neighbors on each side. Then she switched on her lapel pin.

"Hunter? It's Jane. Where are you?"

She waited for an answer as long as she dared. She repeated the message twice more, flushing each time to create more noise. Other people came and went. When she realized that Hunter could not or would not respond, she gave up and left the rest room. Now she was really alone.

Out in the main room again, she heard the rumbling of trucks outside. Everyone else gradually began moving toward the front door. She wanted to stay here, where Hunter could find her, but she did not dare risk attracting attention. To avoid that, she would have to stay with everyone else.

No one else spoke very much. Everyone plodded patiently out to one specific truck and climbed into the back, where picks and shovels were stored in barrels. For them, of course, this was an established routine.

Jane boarded also and soon found herself standing shoulder to shoulder with the other women out in the cold, clear winter morning. Their truck, part of a convoy, jerked and moved away. The convoy wound through the streets of Moscow, stopping at other large buildings that had been converted to emergency housing. When all the trucks were full, they snaked out along an unpaved highway to the west.

All the women in the work brigade were well bundled against the cold. Jane could not remember if Judy had told her how long they had been doing this. No snow lay on the ground right now, but Jane could tell by the way the truck bounced and rumbled on the unpaved road that the mud was frozen solid. At one point, she overheard a woman say that the temperature was about minus twenty centigrade.

Finally Jane saw the ditches appear in the distance. As the convoy turned to run parallel to them, heading for the ends still under construction, Jane looked down at them. She estimated that the nearest ditches were about eight meters wide and three or four meters deep.

When the truck creaked to a halt, Jane jumped to the ground with the others and accepted a shovel from someone. No one told her what to do, so she followed the other women. They walked down an earthen ramp into the middle of the ditch.

Some women stood in the center of the ditch, digging the deepest groove. They moved dirt to an intermediate ledge, where other women shoveled it up to the surface. There, a few more women began arranging the dirt into a ridge on each side of the ditch to make the ditch seem even deeper.

Relatively few men were in the brigade. The ones Jane could see were either too old for the military or else injured in some way. The men took picks to the undisturbed, frozen ground at each end of the ditch and began to break it loose.

Jane could see that the purpose of the brigade was to create a ditch big enough and steep enough that German tanks would go front-down into them so sharply that they could not roll forward to come up the other side. Jane picked out a spot a short distance from the other women and switched on her lapel pin. That way, at least, she would hear Hunter in the unlikely event that he called her, despite their agreement that he should not risk it. Right now, it was her best hope. Then she started to dig. If nothing else, the activity helped her keep warm.

Hunter chose to return at midday following the night he left. As before, he took his team to a spot outside the city to avoid being noticed on their arrival. They landed east of Moscow, on the opposite side of the city from the front. He hoped that would help them avoid army patrols from either side.

"You going to call Jane?" Steve asked. "I'm worried about her."

"I do not dare, at least until taking the risk becomes justified," said Hunter. "I am not receiving any sound from her, which means she has either turned off her lapel pin or else she is out of range. I calculate the chance of her being surrounded by other people to be extremely high. If her lapel pin is turned off or out of range, calling her will not matter. If it is turned on and within range, I would risk attracting attention."

"Wait a minute," said Steve. "She's been through this long enough to know how it works. If it's turned on, that means she figures it's safe to hear from you."

"At this time I will not take the risk," said Hunter. "We must walk back to the warehouse and see if she is there." He pointed toward the city.

"Look that way," said Judy, pointing north as they began to walk.

Hunter saw a faint, dark line on the horizon, too vague to identify. "Do you know what that is?"

"The Sixteenth and Twentieth Soviet armies are encamped that direction," said Judy. "They'll be opening the counterattack soon, to drive the Germans back from Moscow. I think we're looking at the very southern end of their line."

"Can they help us in any way?" Hunter asked.

Judy shook her head emphatically. "No. The military has political commissars all through it."

"They are as unpredictable as the NKVD?"

"Well . . . let's just say that the potential exists all through the Soviet system. We should avoid all the authorities as much as possible."

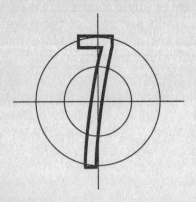

Wayne sat huddled with Ishihara alone in a small two-man tent. The night before, the patrol had taken them to a Leutnant Johann Mohr. Leutnant Mohr had communicated with them in rather limited English. Then he had tried to contact his Hauptmann, who put him off until this morning; Ishihara explained that the Hauptmann was the German equivalent of captain. So Wayne and Ishihara had been put into this tent for the night, under guard.

To keep his guests away from the soldiers, Leutnant Mohr had ordered one of his men to bring their breakfast to the tent, maintaining their isolation. Wayne was finishing his bowl of hot gruel. Ishihara had already put his aside. For now, they were simply left to wait. Wayne felt certain that Leutnant Mohr was afraid to take responsibility for making any decision regarding them.

"We'll have to continue faking our way with some kind of background story," said Wayne quietly. "Will this be acceptable to you under the Laws of Robotics?"

"Yes," said Ishihara. "The First Law requires that I keep you safe as I aid your mission. To do so, we must convince our hosts that we belong."

Finally the flap of the tent was drawn back and Leutnant Mohr leaned down to look inside. He was a tall, slender young man with blondish brown hair. His stained gray uniform was torn in several places but had been brushed free of surface dirt. "Hauptmann Eber will see you now," he said in heavily accented English. "Come now."

Wayne crawled out of the tent and wrapped his cloak tightly around him again. As he and Ishihara followed Leutnant Mohr, the soldiers who had been guarding them fell into step around them. Leutnant Mohr had been courteous to Wayne and Ishihara, in case they were telling the truth, but he had taken no chances, either.

As they walked among the rows of tents, Wayne could see that the German army around him was in poor shape. Supplies and equipment were stacked on farm and peasant carts pulled by little horses with fuzzy winter coats. These vehicles, in fact, were smaller and more poorly maintained than the wagons in the Roman baggage train back in A.D. 9.

The soldiers around them had not shaved, mended their clothes or boots, or washed with soap. Many were obviously very ill, coughing and wheezing in the cold air. A large number also had dirty bandages on wounds that had apparently not been sufficiently serious to warrant sending them to the rear. Suddenly Wayne realized that Leutnant Mohr and his men had no winter coats or boots. He turned to look around at the other soldiers in the camp, and saw no sign of winter clothing anywhere.

Leutnant Mohr brought them to an officer standing over a metal barrel, in which a small fire burned. He was a burly man with a full face and several days' growth of brown beard. His face was taut against the cold wind.

Leutnant Mohr saluted and spoke to his Hauptmann in German, then turned to Wayne and Ishihara. "Hauptmann Uwe Eber."

Hauptmann Eber spoke to Wayne in German, staring at Wayne grimly. Leutnant Mohr translated into English.

"You are Swedish? Why are you speaking English?" Hauptmann Eber frowned.

"Ishihara and I have only English as a common language," said Wayne. "And Ishihara can speak German with Leutnant Mohr, but I can't. Leutnant Mohr and I also share English."

Hauptmann Eber nodded, listening to the translation. "Why would a Swede be here on the Russian front?"

"I am Swedish, but partial to your cause. My friend and I are working with Swedish intelligence."

"Are you?" Hauptmann Eber turned his icy gaze on Ishihara. "Leutnant Mohr says you are Japanese? You are clearly not Japanese. What is this nonsense?"

"I am not Japanese," said Ishihara. "I lived in Japan for many years and took the name of my host family out of respect for them. This is why I have a Japanese name and also why my German and my knowledge of Europe are flawed."

"What is your purpose here?"

"We have come to the front in order to locate a Russian spy who may have infiltrated the German front," said Ishihara, in a confident, businesslike tone.

For the first time, Hauptmann Eber's face registered concern. His eyes widened momentarily, then he studied Ishihara's face. Without looking away, he spoke sharply to Leutnant Mohr, who saluted, turned, and hurried off alone.

Hauptmann Eber did not speak. He looked around the camp and patiently warmed his hands over the little fire. The soldiers in Leutnant Mohr's escort edged closer to the fire, eyeing the captain warily.

"He has sent Leutnant Mohr to find his own superior," Ishihara said quietly in English to Wayne. "A Major Bach."

Wayne nodded. "He's just like Mohr. Nobody wants to take any responsibility for us. They keep going up the line of command."

"This system works on fear," said Ishihara. "The punishment for making mistakes is severe. It helps to focus authority at the top, where this government wants power to gather."

In a few minutes, Leutnant Mohr came trotting back. He stopped and saluted. He and Hauptmann Eber exchanged a few quick words in German. Then Leutnant Mohr switched to English again.

"Major Bach has suggested that we all meet in Oberst Schepke's command tent."

Ishihara nodded politely. "*Ja.*"

"Just as you were saying," said Wayne, with a slight grin, as they turned and began to walk.

"Which rank are we going to see now?"

"Oberst is the equivalent of colonel," said Ishihara.

In the command tent, Wayne stood patiently as all the German officers reported in German to their Oberst. Major Bach was a short, burly man with dark hair. Oberst Schepke, a scowling, gaunt, hawk-nosed man, stood formally behind a battered wooden table, listening and asking questions. Then he used Leutnant Mohr as an interpreter to speak to his visitors.

"The Oberst has ordered me to use English so that both of you can understand," said Leutnant Mohr, turning to face Wayne and Ishihara. "He requires your credentials."

Wayne felt a surge of panic. He could not think of anything to say. Worried, he glanced at Ishihara.

"You misunderstand," Ishihara said, with a formality and stiffness that matched those of the Oberst. "We are undercover, traveling across the national boundaries of many nations. Certainly we could not operate effectively against the Russian spy we seek if we carried documents that would expose our true mission."

"Then present whatever travel documents you have. You must have passports of some sort."

"They were taken from us and not returned," said Ishihara smoothly.

"By whom?"

"By petty bureaucrats in Switzerland."

Wayne was impressed. Ishihara was demonstrating a deft ability to improvise. Wayne assumed he was drawing on his limited history of this time.

"I must have some way to verify your identity," Leutnant Mohr said for Oberst Schepke.

"Field Marshal Mannstein will speak for us," said Ishihara coolly.

Wayne had never heard of him.

"Mannstein," repeated the Oberst, showing some surprise as he recognized the name without translation. Then he spoke to Leutnant Mohr in German again.

"Contacting Mannstein from here will take some time. He is still on the Finnish border, moving on Leningrad," Leutnant Mohr translated.

Wayne suppressed a smile. That was probably why Ishihara had picked that particular individual as a reference. Also, of course, Finland was next to Sweden, where Wayne had supposedly originated. That might help convince Oberst Schepke that Mannstein was a legitimate reference.

"We do not have time to waste," said Ishihara, maintaining his calm, reserved delivery. "The spy we seek came this way. He is probably among us now, observing conditions and positions on our front. Soon, however, he will head for the Soviet lines to report what he has found."

"How much do you know about him? Do you know his appearance and what name he is using?"

"We know exactly what he looks like. We don't know what he is calling himself."

"You have a photograph? Give it to me."

"Our photograph has been lost on our travels. We have journeyed far, and quickly, to get here."

"Then describe him."

Ishihara described the short, slender component robot, who was physically identical to the
other five who comprised MC Governor in com-
bination with him.

Oberst Schepke was silent, looking at Ishihara
and Wayne thoughtfully. Then he spoke again,
nodding at their clothing. Leutnant Mohr continued to translate.

"Why are you dressed this way?"

"We have had to travel alone, with little money
and no support, through much of Europe. In the
wild mountains of Carpathia, our normal traveling
clothes were reduced to rags. We accepted these
clothes from Slavic peasants in a remote mountain
village, where civilization has barely reached."

"Yes. I have seen such places. We have no clothes
to spare here, either."

Ishihara nodded his acknowledgment. "Oberst,
may we get on with our task? This spy must not be
allowed to report your positions to the enemy."

Oberst Schepke studied Ishihara for a long
moment without speaking. Wayne could see that
he was torn between the fear of a spy in his
camp and the fact that his visitors had no proof
to back up their story. The Oberst, too, had to
fear the reprisals of his own superiors if he made
a mistake—regarding either possibility. Then he
spoke again, briefly.

"Leutnant Mohr—that is, I—will escort you
about the lines within the area under my command," Leutnant Mohr translated. "If your quest
leads you into the command of another Oberst,
you must return to me for an introduction."

"Thank you, Oberst," said Ishihara.

Oberst Schepke nodded sharply and barked an order. All the soldiers snapped to attention, angled their right arms up, palms forward, and spoke in unison: *"Heil Hitler."*

The soldiers did an about-face and marched out, but Oberst Schepke eyed Wayne and Ishihara suspiciously.

Suddenly Ishihara imitated the salute. Following his lead, so did Wayne. *"Heil Hitler."*

Ishihara followed the soldiers out and Wayne stayed close to him. Outside the tent, Wayne let out a long sigh and relaxed for the first time since they had walked in. Most of the soldiers dispersed, but Leutnant Mohr remained.

"You were slow with the salute, my friends," said Leutnant Mohr, looking pointedly at both of them.

"I fear, Leutnant, that we are out of practice," said Ishihara. "As intelligence officers in neutral countries, and sometimes behind enemy lines, we must be careful not to speak too quickly."

Leutnant Mohr shrugged uncomfortably. "Where shall we begin? Do you have a particular place?"

"No," said Ishihara. "Let us start simply by walking through the lines, asking questions of the soldiers. As we go, I shall describe our quarry to you. Perhaps he can be found among refugees or POWs."

"Very well."

As they began to explore the lines, Wayne surmised how Oberst Schepke had made his decision. Finding the spy was too important to ignore. Since only his visitors could identify him, they had to be given some chance to do so.

At the same time, he could not allow the strangers to wander around his camp unsupervised. Wayne also suspected that the Oberst had decided not to assign a higher ranking officer for this, for fear he would be embarrassed later if their story was not true. Yet he could not trust an enlisted man with this task. For that reason, as well as his ability to speak English, Leutnant Mohr had received the chore.

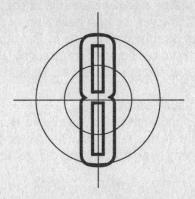

Hunter knew that the walk back into Moscow was a long one for his human companions. Even he was using more energy than the weak winter sun could restore on the microscopic solar power cells in his skin. The activity helped keep the humans warm, but they needed a rest by the time they reached the edge of the city.

He did not see a place nearby where they could get warm. They settled for a bench on a sidewalk. A few other Muscovites walked past them.

"We should be able to find a bus line, I think," said Judy. "I think some of them are still running."

"Excellent," said Hunter.

"Hunter," said Steve. "Where are you going to look for MC 4, anyhow?"

"Not too far from here," said Hunter. "My calculation of where MC 4 will likely return to his full size is out in a certain neighborhood that I will show you. He should return within a range of a couple of blocks."

"After we find Jane, then, are we just going to stake out the area?"

"That will be a good beginning, of course," said Hunter. "However, he may have already returned, or he may simply slip past us as the other component robots have on earlier missions. If we lose him that way, our search will be even more difficult than before."

"Why?" Judy asked.

"He has more places to hide," said Hunter. "In the middle of this large city, he can find shelter and company fairly quickly and can get lost in the crowds."

"He won't have a job or a place to live," said Steve. "And when he first shows up, he won't even have any clothes. That will make him stand out in a crowd."

Judy laughed.

"Clothes can be found in a city," said Hunter. "Further, with so many displaced people, I believe that fewer questions are being routinely asked of strangers than usual."

"That's right," said Judy.

"Yeah, I see," said Steve. "In the dinosaur age, all we had to do was find MC 1's footprints or broken twigs to pick up his trail. And even in Port Royal, Jamaica, and on the Roman frontier, a single stranger was pretty obvious to everybody. This is a much more sophisticated urban area, isn't it?"

"Yes," said Judy emphatically. "And, remember, the government is very dangerous. Don't underestimate them."

"Got it," said Steve. "Hunter, I'm starting to get cold, just sitting here."

"Judy, are you rested enough to continue?" Hunter asked.

"Might as well get it over with."

"We shall look at the area where I expect MC 4 to appear on our way back to the warehouse," said Hunter, rising.

"Let's look for a major thoroughfare," said Judy. "The city has reduced bus service, but the biggest streets will have what's left."

As they began to walk again, Judy looked up and down the blocks and suggested directions. Soon they were in a queue at a bus stop behind seven Muscovites. When the bus to the center of the city arrived, it was a very old, creaking vehicle puffing black smoke out of its exhaust pipe. As Hunter led his team into the bus, he imitated the woman in front of him, paying the team's way with coins. The bus was only half-full, so they found seats in the rear, away from other people.

Hunter sat without speaking, looking out the windows. When he saw that the bus had reached the area where he had estimated MC 4 would appear, he stood up and pulled the horizontal cord running across the wall of the bus over the windows. A little bell rang by the driver, who pulled over at the next bus stop.

Hunter gestured for Judy and Steve to leave the rear door first. When they were safely on the sidewalk again, he followed them. The bus creaked and rumbled away, blowing black smoke over them into the chilly air.

"Doesn't look like much, does it?" Judy looked up and down the street.

"What kind of buildings are these?" Hunter asked, surveying the architecture.

"These are all residential apartment buildings. Most of them are empty in the daytime."

"Where is everybody?" Steve asked.

"Oh, you missed my explanation before, didn't you?" Judy turned to him. "Men who can serve in the military left a long time ago and lots of people have fled to avoid the advancing Germans. I think that's where many of the children went; families got them out of town. The remainder are working overtime to keep the city functioning or to prepare defenses."

"That means MC 4 could appear here and duck into a fairly empty building, doesn't it?" Steve looked up at the rows of windows in the building above them.

"Yes," said Hunter. "He can also find clothing, if he locates something he judges the owner can lose without harm."

"We can't knock on every door," said Steve. "What do you want to do?"

"I do not have a plan yet," said Hunter. "I fear that finding him here will be difficult. We shall not be able to watch this area constantly without attracting the notice of the authorities."

"That's right," said Judy.

"I want to find Jane," said Steve. "Then we can concentrate on MC 4."

Hunter magnified his hearing to the maximum, listening for footsteps suggesting the weight of MC 4, or his voice speaking English. He turned slowly in different directions, but heard no signs of the component robot. This failure meant very little, however, considering the density and size of the buildings. MC 4 could be quite close, or could still be microscopic, or might have already left the area at full size.

"I agree, Steve," said Hunter. "We shall remain here at this bus stop and find a bus going toward the warehouse to look for Jane."

"Is the NKVD looking for you two?" Steve asked. "You think they'll go back to the warehouse?"

"It is possible," said Hunter. "Since I have changed my appearance back to normal, they will not recognize me. However, they did see Judy clearly."

"We'd better sleep somewhere else tonight," said Steve, looking up the street. "How much time is there between buses, anyway, Judy?"

"I'm afraid I don't know. That's too much detail for the history I studied."

Hunter looked at her. "Once we get there, Judy will have to hide in the crowd in case the NKVD returns. We shall leave as soon as we have Jane with us again. Please be very careful and very aware of people noticing you."

"Count on it," said Judy, smiling wryly. "I've seen enough of them already. I'll be careful."

By the time the sun was low on the flat western horizon, Jane was already exhausted. For the last couple of hours, she had shoveled slowly, with very little dirt on the blade of her shovel. As long as she continued moving, however, no one else in the work brigade seemed to care.

She had not been able to get enough privacy to call Hunter. Except in the outhouse, which had no water to flush, she had not been alone all day. She had not dared use her lapel pin for fear of being overheard by the people waiting in line outside.

During the course of the day, the ditch had grown. Since Judy had told the team that the Battle of Moscow would involve the Soviet armies counterattacking the Germans, Jane knew that the ditch she was digging was probably not important. She knew she was not altering history by participating.

Finally she heard the rumble of trucks. Everyone looked up to see the welcome sight. She fell into line with the others, climbing out of the ditch and queuing for the ride back to the warehouse.

In the back of the truck as it jerked and drove away, Jane leaned against the side and slid down to a sitting position. She had not been this tired in a long time. As a roboticist, she was simply not used to an entire day of the kind of physical labor that robots would do in her time. The cold had taken a toll on her, as well; the daytime temperature here had been much colder than even the mountains of central Germany on their previous mission.

Even when the truck finally stopped, she did not stand right away. She waited while the back was opened and the rest of the work brigade began to climb out. Finally she stood up, stiff with the cold, and followed them out of the truck.

Jane joined the crowd moving toward the door of the warehouse. Then she glanced up and saw Hunter just inside the door, towering over the others. A wave of relief swept over her, but she knew better than to call out. To those around her, she had to look as resigned as they were about this difficult routine. As before, two burly men stood by the door, watching as everyone entered. When she finally got inside, she could see Judy and Steve for the first time.

"Good evening," Steve said in Russian, grinning. "You okay?"

"Worn out," said Jane. "How did you get here? Hunter, where have you been all this time?"

"We can confer in a moment," said Hunter. "Now we must leave the warehouse."

"All right." Jane accepted his judgment. "I'm ready."

Hunter, moving against the current of people still plodding into the warehouse, slipped around the edge of the doorway. Steve waited for Jane and Judy to file after him, so Jane pushed her way after Hunter.

"Where are you going, comrade?" One of the guards put his hand against Hunter's chest.

"We must find some friends," said Hunter. "Please excuse us." He started to moved around the man, but the guard shifted with him, still blocking the way.

"It is dark, comrade, and cold. Come inside for the night." He gestured back toward the doorway.

"This is very important," said Hunter.

"Then you must explain it to me."

Hunter hesitated, then glanced over his shoulder at his team. Then he moved back inside. Hunter led the team back to the familiar corner in the rear of the warehouse. Jane and Steve exchanged puzzled glances but did not argue.

"What's wrong, Hunter?" Jane spoke quietly, seeing that no strangers were close to them. "We have to get out of here."

"The NKVD knows what Judy looks like now and may return here for her," said Hunter. "We cannot risk remaining here."

"Exactly," said Steve. "We could have rushed out of here. You could have pushed past that guy."

"I do not want to force our way out past the guards, either," said Hunter. "That would be disruptive and would attract even more attention to us."

"You aren't just going to sit here and wait for the NKVD," said Steve. "So what *are* we going to do?"

"For now, please prepare to sleep," said Hunter. "I shall consider the options that we shall have after the lights are out."

Wayne let Ishihara do most of the work in their day's search. He knew that Ishihara could turn up the sensitivity of his sight and hearing to find MC 4 and nothing Wayne could do was the equal of that. So he spent most of his time just holding his cloak as tight as he could.

Leutnant Mohr rarely spoke as he dutifully led his guests through the tents and up and down the lines. Wayne became sure that the Nazi command had ordered Leutnant Mohr to be very careful with them. If they proved legitimate, then Oberst Schepke wanted to be able to prove later that he had cooperated with them fully. At the same time, he wanted to distance himself from the strangers in case they were phony. As a result, Leutnant Mohr did not spend much time talking to soldiers or letting them see inside tents. He gave them a perfunctory tour of the grounds that did not accomplish very much.

At one point late in the day, Ishihara stopped and looked east. Wayne saw only open, frozen ground. He waited to see what Ishihara would do.

"Lieutenant," said Ishihara, in English.

"Yes?"

"How far is the actual front line?"

"This encampment is roughly a half kilometer from the front," said Leutnant Mohr, squinting into the distance himself. "We are in Panzer Group 3, a mere twenty kilometers or so from Moscow itself."

"Straight east of here?" Ishihara asked.

"So we are told."

"How long since anybody moved?" Wayne asked.

"Excuse me?" Leutnant Mohr stiffened.

"How long have you held this position, without advancing?" Wayne turned to look at him pointedly.

"We are searching for a spy, not discussing military matters." Leutnant Mohr fidgeted uncomfortably.

"Lieutenant." Wayne used his most authoritative tone of voice and tried to think like one of the German military men. "I want to know if that spy is gaining information of value—how fresh it is, or how old. It bears directly on our purpose. Now answer my question."

"Well—the front moved slowly during the fall. The camp doesn't move as often, of course. We advance the camp after the front is secure."

Wayne looked around again. He could see the German tanks lined up in rows, sitting cold, with their crews huddled around small fires. Certainly no orders to move up had gone out today. This army looked to him as if it was freezing in place.

"Have you received any orders about advancing?" Ishihara asked.

"We have been told we will spend the winter in Moscow," Leutnant Mohr said cautiously. His young face looked unsure as he glanced toward the empty horizon again.

Wayne caught Ishihara's glance and understood the point behind his question. They had come here because Wayne had expected MC 4 to attempt stopping the German advance. Wayne considered it a likely imperative under the First Law. However, if the German offensive had already stalled, then MC 4 had no need to influence them.

MC 4 might not be here at all.

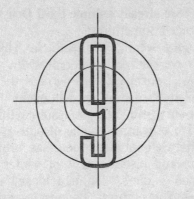

Late in the afternoon, Wayne decided to let Leutnant Mohr off the hook for a while and requested that he and Ishihara take a rest. Leutnant Mohr left them in his own tent, with a firm suggestion that they remain there while he tended to his other duties. Wayne saw that he posted a couple of guards outside the tent as he left.

Wayne moved close to Ishihara and spoke quietly.

"We aren't accomplishing much here."

"I agree," said Ishihara.

"Do you have any ideas?"

"I have some information."

"You do?"

"Yes. I have been monitoring the German radio communications continuously."

"What did you find out?"

"From the communications among middle-rank and senior officers coordinating their daily routines, I have learned that Panzer Group 3 is in fact blocked on its way to Moscow by the Soviet Red Army."

"Didn't we already assume that? Or is it a military secret or something?"

"It is not a secret," said Ishihara. "The German officers have referred to it repeatedly. However, until now, I surmised that perhaps the German army had stopped from exhaustion."

Wayne shrugged. "Did you learn anything else?"

"Yes. I overheard a couple of officers in effect saying that General Alfried Jodl has forbidden the collection and disbursement of winter clothing to German soldiers." Ishihara looked at Wayne carefully. "This information puzzles me. It also disturbs me under the First Law."

"That sounds weird to me, too. Why would he do that? Do you know?"

"According to the officers whom I overheard, this general fears that providing winter clothing to their soldiers would cast doubt on his guarantee that they will take Moscow before the onset of winter and spend the season safely in the city."

"You mean he's leaving them in the cold so they'll be more confident of taking Moscow soon?"

"That seems to be their belief, yes."

"That's why they're all freezing? Not because the German command can't get the winter clothes— because they refuse to?"

"Yes. That is a critical reason that the German soldiers are suffering so much from the weather."

Wayne nodded slowly. "Did you overhear anything else important?"

"No." Ishihara lowered his voice even more. "I cannot stop thinking about the harm being done to all these men. They should all simply go home.

Then no more war would take place on this front."

"Even if they did, the Russians would chase them, wouldn't they? And keep fighting."

"Yes, that is what happened. As I access what limited history I have, I see also that the Nazi government is very cruel and oppressive, and that this mind-set has influenced many soldiers. The leadership is very destructive and survives on terror."

"Not every soldier can be like that," said Wayne. "Most of them must be ordinary people."

"These individuals are emotionally broken past the point of taking their own initiative. The higher ranks keep their lives and positions by cooperating—following orders, no matter what they are. So do their subordinates."

"What are we going to do?"

"I do not have precise details about this particular site in the war," said Ishihara. "However, from the condition of the German army, I believe that the military initiative lies with the Soviet army."

"Then you think we should go to the other side to look for MC 4?"

"Quite possibly. If he reaches the same conclusion, then he might try to stop the battle by interfering with the Soviet side in some way."

"Okay," said Wayne thoughtfully. "But how do we get across the front to the other side—without both sides shooting at us?"

"I propose that we continue our charade," said Ishihara. "As agents in pursuit of an enemy spy."

"How so?"

"We could offer to infiltrate the enemy. If we suggest, for instance, that MC 4 has already returned to the enemy to brief them on the information he has gathered, then it would be natural for us to follow him."

"I see. Maybe the Germans would help us get across, at least part of the way."

"We must be careful in presenting this idea to our hosts," said Ishihara.

"Yeah, you're right about that," said Wayne. "These Nazis are still suspicious of us."

"We cannot allow them to doubt us any more than they do already."

"How do you want to handle this?"

"I suggest we drop hints," said Ishihara. "Our best opportunity may lie in inducing our hosts to make this suggestion."

"All right," said Wayne. "Let's get our story straight before Mohr comes back."

"We are too late," said Ishihara. "I hear his footsteps coming now."

Before Wayne could reply, he heard the footsteps too. Leutnant Mohr threw back the flap of the tent. Cold wind blew inside as he stooped to enter.

"It never gets any warmer," said Leutnant Mohr.

"That's true," said Wayne. "But we've been talking about our mission."

Leutnant Mohr sat down, wrapping his arms around himself. "It is good to get out of the wind."

Wayne nodded. He felt that Leutnant Mohr seemed uncomfortable with the informality. For a moment, no one spoke.

"Our spy may already have left the area," said Ishihara, in a calm, unconcerned tone.

"Yes?" Leutnant Mohr fumbled ostentatiously at his shirt pockets for a moment, then sighed. "Do either of you have a cigarette, by any chance?"

"A what?" Wayne asked.

"We do not," said Ishihara quickly. "I apologize. We have often been deprived during our travels."

Leutnant Mohr nodded.

"Cigarettes are very harmful," Ishihara added.

"So's the Red Army." Leutnant Mohr grinned crookedly.

"We do not know how far ahead of us the enemy spy may be," said Ishihara.

"We think we're pretty close behind him," Wayne added, hoping to help Ishihara.

Leutnant Mohr nodded noncommittally. "Your fur cloaks look primitive, but I suppose they are warm."

"Yes, that is true," said Ishihara. "Your uniform is not really heavy enough for this Russian climate, is it? You must be very cold."

"It is nothing." Leutnant Mohr stiffened suddenly, shrugging. "We shall be in Moscow soon."

"Not if our quarry has reached it already," said Wayne, in what he hoped was as casual a tone as Ishihara was using. "That's what we've been talking about."

"Yes?" Leutnant Mohr glanced at him, more interested.

"He may have already learned enough about German positions to brief his masters."

"So soon?"

"This is possible," said Ishihara. "With the German army stationary now, the Soviet Army would gain information that will remain reliable until we move again."

"You mean you're too late?" Leutnant Mohr's eyes were wide. "The Russians already know our positions?"

"Not necessarily," said Wayne. "We may be very close behind him."

"We believe we can stop him," said Ishihara.

"What do you think?" Wayne looked directly into the Leutnant's blue eyes.

"You must catch him at all costs."

Wayne decided that Mohr was not going to take the bait directly. "We may need to chase him across the front into the city. Can you help?"

Leutnant Mohr's back straightened. His voice became formal and cautious. "I must return you to Hauptmann Eber for that sort of question."

"Can we cut short the process a little this time?" Wayne asked. "Instead of going to Hauptmann Eber and then the Major and then Oberst Schepke—can we just go talk to the Oberst right away?"

Leutnant Mohr shook his head tightly. "No! It is not done. I must report to my immediate superior."

"All right." Wayne sighed. "We certainly don't want to get you into trouble. Take us to your Hauptmann, please."

Leutnant Mohr nodded and led them out of the tent.

In the early evening wind, Wayne wrapped his cloak more tightly around him. The pale sun went down as he and Ishihara followed the Leutnant through the camp. As before, Hauptmann Eber took them to Major Bach, who was squatting outside his tent, warming himself over a small fire in the gathering gloom.

Hauptmann Eber spoke briefly to the Major in German. Instead of insisting immediately that they confer with Oberst Schepke, however, Major Bach listened to their argument in full. He did not bother to stand. As before, Leutnant Mohr acted as interpreter.

"I don't know, Hauptmann," said Major Bach slowly. The firelight played off his face, making him look mysterious in the shadows. "What do you think? If this spy has already left, then it's too late to catch him. He will be debriefed as soon as he arrives, will he not?"

"Most likely, sir."

"He is on foot," said Ishihara.

"Oh? And how do you know?" Major Bach asked, turning to slightly to face him.

"As far as we know, that is the case," said Ishihara politely. "Since he must avoid notice from our sentries, he has to be very careful in leaving the camp and maneuvering around German military lines."

"What of it?" Major Bach spoke in a tone of complete indifference.

"He must also worry about approaching Soviet lines, to avoid being shot coming across the front."

"He will have some sort of contact or credentials, or some identifying information." Hauptmann Eber, apparently sensing the Major's skeptical tone, folded his arms and glared at Ishihara. "More than you have, I might add."

"If he is shot before he arrives, that will not matter," said Ishihara. "He must find a way to make contact with someone on the other side before they open fire. All of this means that he must move slowly—not to mention that he has roughly twenty kilometers of open ground between the two armies to cross somehow."

"You think he is going to walk twenty kilometers to Moscow?"

"The German infantry has walked much farther than that already."

Major Bach nodded. "I presume you wish help in pursuing him, not just permission to leave us."

"We feel it is worth the risk," said Ishihara. "If he left this camp today, for instance, then we may still be able to catch him before he locates his superiors, whether or not he reaches Moscow ahead of us. Even a small amount of help would make a difference."

Major Bach gazed quietly into the fire without speaking. Following his lead, Hauptmann Eber did the same. Leutnant Mohr watched them both, his eyes shifting between them nervously.

Wayne waited, expecting that the Major would finally abdicate responsibility after all, and take them back to Oberst Schepke.

Finally Major Bach spoke briefly over his shoulder to an aide, who hurried into a tent. Then he spoke to Wayne and Ishihara again. "I will write you a pass to leave the camp. It can be countermanded by someone of higher rank, of course, but I trust you will not trouble anyone of that sort." He eyed them both pointedly.

"Of course," said Wayne.

"Thank you, Major," said Ishihara.

"You will be on your own, however. I cannot spare men or supplies to help you."

Wayne said nothing. Crossing the front to Moscow was going to be difficult without a vehicle. He had hoped the Major would offer them some help. Since Ishihara was not debating the point, Wayne decided to keep quiet, too.

The aide brought a pen and a slip of paper to the Major. Wayne realized that Major Bach was making a decision similar to the one Oberst Schepke had made about them earlier. The Major wanted to appear cooperative, in case they were legitimate, but he did not want to give them any real help, in case they were not.

Further, Major Bach did not want to trouble his own superior about them again. After all, Oberst Schepke had accepted their story, however cautiously. Now Major Bach had apparently decided that getting rid of them in this way fell within the scope of his own authority. Once Wayne and Ishihara were gone, these officers could forget about them and focus on military matters again. Maybe most important of all in this suffering army, they would not have to feed and shelter these two noncombatants.

Major Bach handed the pass to his aide, who in turn gave it to Ishihara.

"Thank you, Major," said Ishihara. "Surely you won't mind if Leutnant Mohr drives us to the edge of camp."

Major Bach stood up for the first time, his face suddenly impatient.

"We will remember your cooperation," Wayne said quickly but calmly.

The Major hesitated, studying his face again. Then his shoulders sagged. "Of course. Leutnant Mohr?" He gestured wearily and then squatted close to the fire again.

Jane huddled in the corner of the warehouse. Gradually, other people around them stretched out to sleep for the night. Soon the overhead lights were turned out, leaving only one lamp burning at a table in the front and a single bare bulb over the rest room door. The two guards talked with a couple of women at the front table. The rear of the warehouse was almost completely dark.

"We must leave before the NKVD agents return here seeking Judy or someone who could tell them where to find her," said Hunter quietly. "The rear door is in almost complete darkness."

"It's quiet in here," said Steve. "As soon as we get up and start moving, those guys in the front will hear us. Especially if the door creaks."

"Yes," said Hunter. "I have been looking for a diversion we can create."

"Do you see something, Hunter?" Jane asked, looking around the shadowed warehouse herself.

"I believe so," said Hunter. "The electrical wiring here is primitive, with the insulated cords along the base of the wall fully exposed. A small door in the wall by the rest room almost certainly houses fuses and circuit breakers."

"What do you have in mind?" Judy asked.

"The circuit breakers can be triggered without any long-term harm to the system or to the safety of the humans here," said Hunter. "If one of us moves the switches, then the light in front will go out."

"Sounds good to me," said Steve. "That should create just enough surprise and confusion for us to slip out the back door. Is that what you want to do?"

"Yes, but we must plan this carefully, since that light bulb will illuminate anyone near the circuit breaker. One of us can go use the rest room without causing undue concern. However, I prefer that I not be the one. I should be near the door in case it must be forced open."

"I'll go," said Judy, glancing around the warehouse. "Steve might attract attention, since he doesn't resemble the Slavic Russians."

"I'll go with you," said Jane. "If we have to improvise, two will be better than one."

"Okay."

"You cannot take your overcoats without being noticed," said Hunter. "I shall carry them and give them to you when we are safely outside."

"I'll take the duffel bag," said Steve.

"All right," said Judy. She got up and began to pick her way directly across the warehouse to the rest room.

Jane stood up and slowly followed Judy. Her heart was pounding with tension, but she moved slowly and casually. They worked their way among the sleeping Russians, careful not to disturb any of them.

When they reached the rest room, Judy turned the knob. Jane saw it move in her hand, but Judy pretended it was locked, shrugging theatrically. They stood patiently, pretending to line up.

Trying to act bored, Jane glanced toward the front table. One of the women there, perhaps distracted by the movement of Jane and Judy, looked up. Then the woman yawned and returned her attention to her companions. No one else had taken any notice of them.

Judy took Jane's arm and pulled her a couple of steps to one side, so that she blocked the front table's view of the circuit breaker. Jane could not see the rear door in the darkness at the back of the warehouse. Hunter and Steve were also invisible, but she supposed they were moving toward the door by now.

The only path from here to the door ran along the wall. They would have to walk in the dark down this side wall, turn at the back corner, and then cross part of the rear wall to reach the door. The floor was clear all the way, since everyone had tried to keep away from the cold exterior walls when choosing places to sleep.

Jane heard a quiet metallic clink as Judy opened the door to the circuit breakers. Then she heard snapping noises and the warehouse darkened. Exclamations of surprise came from the front. Then a chair scraped on the floor as someone got up to find the problem.

"Around the wall," Jane whispered frantically. "Come on, quick."

Jane hated walking blindly, but trailing one hand on the side wall in the darkness kept her oriented. She held her other arm out in front of her so that she wouldn't bump into the rear wall. Judy shuffled behind her.

Just as Jane's hand touched the rear wall, she heard the door creak. Only a slip of pale moonlight revealed the doorway. She walked faster now that she could see it, and recognized the silhouettes of Hunter and Steve as they moved soundlessly outside.

"Close that door!" One of the men who had been sitting at the front table shouted from about halfway across the room behind them, as he neared the circuit breaker.

More people murmured in the warehouse, disturbed by the shout. Jane ran for the doorway and ducked out; Hunter was bracing it open with one foot while he held Steve's overcoat out for him to take. Judy followed right behind Jane.

"Follow me," Hunter whispered firmly. He turned and took off at a jog.

Jane saw the other overcoats bundled under his arm. She and Judy would have to wait to put them on. Jane ran after Hunter, instantly cold in the frigid night air. They ran through a narrow alley in the dark, silent city. Alongside them, light suddenly came on around the edges of the blackened windows.

"Who's out there?" One of the guards yelled from the rear door. "The city is under curfew! Where are you going? Come back here!"

Hunter turned at the corner of another alley. He waited for Jane and Judy to catch up; Steve brought up the rear. Hunter shook out two over-coats and threw them over the shoulders of the women. Then, instead of moving toward the street, Hunter led them up the other alley.

Jane, holding the coat awkwardly over her shoulders as she ran, wondered if anyone was chasing them. She didn't hear anything. The team turned another corner. Then Hunter stopped, merely a looming shadow in front of Jane, as everyone gathered around him.

"I hear no pursuit," Hunter said quietly, as he put on his own overcoat. "We must not linger for long, but you may pause to catch your breath. Judy, do you think someone will chase us farther?"

"I have no idea," said Judy, shucking her over-coat and throwing her arms into the sleeves. She shrugged it back onto her shoulders. "We'd better assume they will. I don't know how important they consider this curfew, or how much authority those guys have. One thing this society stifles very hard is personal initiative."

"You mean if they weren't told to report or chase people who break the curfew, they won't do anything?" Steve asked, between rasping breaths. He had the duffel bag slung over one shoulder.

"It's unlikely," said Judy. "But they might have been given such orders."

Jane had her own coat on properly now and fumbled the scarf out of her coat pocket with stiff fingers.

"Come on," said Hunter. As before, he jogged up another shadowed alley.

Still holding her scarf, Jane ran after him. As before, they still turned corners frequently, always keeping to back alleys. Finally, Hunter led them out of an alley onto a deserted side street. In the open space, the weak moonlight illuminated their surroundings a little better than before. Hunter stopped and waited for his team to catch their breath again.

"Hunter?" Jane asked, tying on her scarf. "Where are we going?"

"I do not know exactly. However, we can certainly find other buildings of the same kind housing other people displaced by the war."

"How do we find one?" Steve asked.

"I am not sure," said Hunter. "Judy, can you suggest a way to do this?"

"Uh—I'm not sure. I have to think about it."

"All right," said Hunter. "In any case, Judy, you will be safe as long as the NKVD agents don't see you. Now that we are away from the warehouse where they first found you, our chances of avoiding them are much improved."

"True," said Judy. "But I think we'd better keep moving—to stay warm if nothing else."

"Use your hearing as we walk," Jane said to Hunter. "On maximum."

"For what?" Hunter asked, leading them down the dark sidewalk. "What am I listening for?"

"The sound of a lot of people sleeping in one big room," said Jane.

"That won't be very loud," said Steve. "Even to you."

"I am turning up my aural sensitivity," said Hunter. "If we come within my hearing range of such sounds, I shall recognize them."

"Good luck," Steve muttered doubtfully.

Wayne and Ishihara followed Leutnant Mohr away from Major Bach's fire. Ishihara had managed to get the Major's permission for the Leutnant to drive them out of the German camp and beyond German lines, but that would still leave many kilometers of open, frozen ground to cross. On the other side, of course, they could expect to find thousands of Soviet soldiers, expecting only the enemy to come across that stretch of territory.

Leutnant Mohr said nothing as he led them to his patrol's armored car. All three of them crowded into the cab. It started with a loud roar and jerked forward.

"How far is it to go past the most forward of the German lines from here?" Ishihara asked casually.

Leutnant Mohr shrugged. "I am not certain. Not far. It will take maybe fifteen minutes, since we must go around so many emplacements."

"Thank you for your courtesy, Leutnant." Ishihara unfastened his fur cloak and shifted in his seat so that he could pull it off.

"You're welcome."

"This cloak is quite warm. With the tunic and our leggings, it is not really necessary for me."

Leutnant Mohr glanced at him in surprise.

Wayne stifled a smile. He was pretty sure he knew where Ishihara was leading. Just in case he was wrong, however, he decided to say nothing until he was sure.

"I might be induced to trade this cloak," said Ishihara, holding a portion of the cloak in front of him where Leutnant Mohr could see it.

"You would trade this cloak?" Leutnant Mohr asked carefully, struggling to hold the wheel as the vehicle bounced across the frozen ground.

"I would consider it."

"I don't have much to trade," said Leutnant Mohr. "What would you want for it?"

"A favor."

"Yes? What is this favor?"

"It will take great courage, Leutnant."

Leutnant Mohr's face tightened. "Are you suggesting that I lack courage?"

"You tell me," said Ishihara.

"What do you want?"

"I want you to drive us across the neutral zone," said Ishihara.

"You mean the no-man's-land?"

"Yes."

"Toward the Red Army? You're insane. We will be blasted into nothing in this armored car."

"Maybe not," said Wayne, feeling that he could participate now. "One car alone will not be mistaken for a major military advance that would get a lot of attention."

"You're both insane."

"As I said, it will take great courage," said Ishihara, in an offhand tone.

Leutnant Mohr said nothing.

"You don't have to shake hands with the Russians," said Wayne. "Just get us as far across the open area to the other side as you can."

"We would have to anticipate enemy patrols," said Leutnant Mohr slowly.

"Most of that terrain is empty," said Wayne. "If we see any sign of the enemy, you can let us get out and then you can run for it."

"That's a long way. I could get into trouble with my superior."

Wayne heard some indecision in the Leutnant's voice for the first time. He took the cloak from Ishihara and reached over to put it on Leutnant Mohr's lap. It was all Wayne could think of to help convince him.

"This is only December," said Ishihara. "Most of the Russian winter still lies ahead."

"We shall take Moscow shortly," said Leutnant. Mohr, just as he had said once before.

"Then you will not need the cloak," said Ishihara. "Please return it."

"Um—wait."

"Yes?" Ishihara hesitated.

"I will do it for both cloaks," said Leutnant Mohr, with sudden firmness.

"What?" Wayne was startled.

"I will drive as close to the Red Army as I can get," said Leutnant Mohr. "In exchange, you will give me your cloak, as well. This is my offer."

Wayne grinned. "There's nothing wrong with his courage, Ishihara. He's just been bargaining with us."

"What is your answer?" Leutnant Mohr asked.

"Sorry," said Wayne. "Ishihara may be warm enough without his cloak, but I won't be. I have to keep mine."

"As you said, it will be a very long walk."

"No deal," said Wayne. "I keep my cloak no matter what. I'll freeze without it."

"One cloak in exchange for the ride," said Ishihara. "Take it or leave it."

"I accept," said Leutnant Mohr.

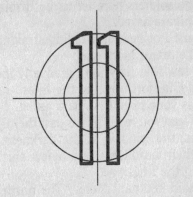

Wayne relaxed, deeply relieved that Leutnant Mohr had given in to their terms. Of course, Leutnant Mohr was as cold as every other soldier in the German army, and the fuel he was using belonged to the army, not to him personally. As he drove, he pulled the heavy fur cloak from Germany, almost two thousand years earlier, over his lap.

Leutnant Mohr was not taking as much of a risk as he believed. Wayne knew that Ishihara would be monitoring the Soviet radio traffic. He would know if any Soviet patrol reported by radio that they were coming this way long before they were in sight.

No one challenged them as they drove close to the most forward German lines. Wayne decided that the entire army was just as cold and discouraged as the soldiers he had seen himself. None of them wanted to take any initiative. As long as the armored car did nothing particularly offensive, he guessed they would not be stopped.

Leutnant Mohr did not immediately drive straight through the lines out into the open front.

"Will the soldiers here let us go through their lines?" Ishihara asked.

"We must not be seen heading straight for the enemy," Leutnant Mohr said.

Wayne saw that they were gradually moving to the left, going north behind the lines.

"What is your plan?" Ishihara asked.

"Yeah—can you really get us past them?" Wayne looked out the window at the darkness, broken only by their headlights and a few small, weak fires along the lines.

"Yes," said Leutnant Mohr. "The north flank is not far. Going out past the flank will mean that we will pass only a few sentries. They may not bother to stop us."

When the armored car finally reached the north flank, Wayne was surprised to see that it was not really anchored in any way. He knew that armies usually wanted some feature in the terrain to protect their flanks, such as a mountain, a river, or even a slight rise in the ground. Here, the German lines simply came to a halt on the level steppe. It was another sign that weariness, cold, and exhaustion had undermined the efficiency of this army.

Suddenly the headlights struck a couple of soldiers waving their arms. Leutnant Mohr sighed and halted their vehicle in front of them. Then he rolled down the window and waited for them to approach him.

One sentry came up to the armored car. He looked at all three of them carefully and then spoke. Wayne could not understand his German, of course, but he could judge the man's tone.

The sentry spoke respectfully, aware that he was addressing an officer. Leutnant Mohr answered quietly and confidently as he handed his pass to him.

The sentry moved so that he could read the pass in the glow of the headlights. He showed it to his partner, who nodded and stepped back. The first sentry returned it to Leutnant Mohr and pointed off into the blackness ahead, saying something else. Then he, too, backed away.

Leutnant Mohr put the vehicle into gear and drove forward, beyond the flank.

"What did they say?" Wayne asked.

"They assumed I was lost," said Leutnant Mohr. "I explained that we were on a special reconnaissance mission and showed them the pass."

"What will you say on the way back?" Wayne asked. "When you're alone?"

"I will circle around this spot and return to the lines farther to the rear. Major Bach's pass will serve with other sentries, who did not see me in your company."

"They must have seen we aren't in uniform," said Wayne. "Did they ask about it?"

"Yes. I told them I was not allowed to reveal your identities."

"Hey, not bad." Wayne grinned. "You're a sharp guy, Leutnant."

Instead of answering, Leutnant Mohr simply pushed the accelerator, taking them faster over the hard ground. They were now moving out into pure darkness slashed only by their own headlights. After a while, he turned to the right.

For the first time, now, they were driving east, toward Moscow and the Soviet lines protecting it. Wayne looked back over his shoulder. The last fires from the German lines were out of sight. That was how Leutnant Mohr had decided the time had come to start across the open area between the lines.

No one spoke for a long time. Wayne could not see the speedometer, if the vehicle had one. In the darkness, he had no way to judge their speed by the passing terrain, either. He did not feel that they were moving very fast, but did not want to raise the subject. At this point, he was just glad they had a ride across the cold, barren countryside.

Wayne glanced up and suddenly realized that he could see powerful beams of light stretching high into the sky in the distance ahead. They started from somewhere on the ground, over the horizon, and swept upward into the sky. He suspected that he should already know what the lights were, so he did not dare ask. Maybe they were looking for enemy aircraft over Moscow. They had probably been visible for some time before he had noticed them.

"I believe we are halfway to enemy lines," Leutnant Mohr said quietly. He did not slow down or turn, but his voice sounded oddly tight.

"We have made excellent progress," said Ishihara. His tone was calm.

Wayne picked up the meaning of his delivery. Ishihara was monitoring the Soviet radio traffic and knew that the Red Army had not noticed them. Leutnant Mohr was getting nervous, though, knowing that they were drawing closer to the enemy than to the safety of his own lines.

They rode in silence for a while longer. Finally, however, Leutnant Mohr came to a stop. Wayne saw nothing in the darkness around them.

"What is wrong?" Ishihara asked.

"We are within five to seven kilometers of enemy lines," said Leutnant Mohr. In the reflected light from the headlights, his face was pale and tense.

"That is still a long walk for us," said Ishihara. "We have had no sign of the enemy."

"This is as far as I dare go," said Leutnant Mohr. "We are certain to attract Soviet patrols in the next few miles. And if they open up with artillery, I will not be able to go back to my own lines quietly, either. I could be blamed for starting an unplanned action."

"But five to seven kilometers," Wayne started. "In this cold, we could—"

"Very well," Ishihara interrupted, speaking more loudly than usual to drown out Wayne. "Your arguments are sound, Leutnant. We thank you for your cooperation."

"I wish you good luck," said Leutnant Mohr.

Wayne and Ishihara got out into the cold night air. The armored car jerked and rumbled away in a large turn. In a moment, it was bouncing over the frozen ground back to the west. Wayne and Ishihara were alone.

"Why didn't you argue a little harder?" Wayne asked, pulling his cloak snugly around him.

"We cannot risk having Leutnant Mohr start a battle prematurely. It could change world history in a manner very destructive to our own time."

Wayne sighed. "Freezing to death will be destructive to me, personally."

"I cannot allow harm to come to you, either. You are already aware of that."

"For that matter, what about you?" Wayne looked at him. "Your energy storage has a limit, too. How long can you manage out here without your cloak?"

"I can pursue normal activity without a problem until dawn, at which time even the weak winter sun will begin to recharge the solar collectors built into my skin surface. Unusually extreme activity tonight could drain me prematurely, but I do not foresee that happening."

"So, we just start walking? I'm not sure I can make it that distance."

"I am certain you cannot," said Ishihara. "I have another plan to propose."

"Good."

"I warn you that considerable risk is involved in this suggestion, too. However, I feel it is less risky to your welfare than simply trying to walk from here would be."

"All right, all right. Get to the point, will you? I'm freezing while we stand here."

"I can radio ahead to the Soviets on my internal system and ask for help."

"Uh—what would you say?"

"We will have to discuss that and come to agreement on our story, just as we did with the Ger-

From the R. Hunter Files

The now-famous prototype of the highly successful "Hunter" class robot first demonstrated his remarkable abilities in the Mojave Center Governor case. The following images are drawn from the Robot City archives of Derec Avery, the eminent historian on robotics.

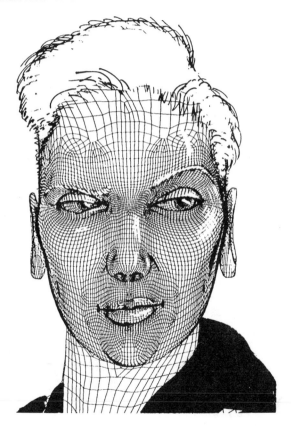

HUNTER IN MOSCOW. R. Hunter's ability to shift his shape to match local conditions proved invaluable on many of his missions. Here Hunter has adopted the disguise of a Russian citizen during World War II.

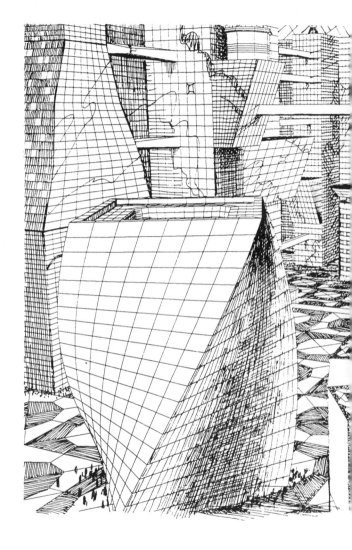

MOJAVE CENTER. In an ambitious attempt to reclaim unusable land and take advantage of readily available solar and wind power, a number of underground cities were built. The state-of-the-art facility under the Mojave Desert, known for its university and famous sculpture gardens, was perhaps the most successful.

WAYNE AND ISHIHARA PURSUED BY THE SECRET POLICE.
Even in wartime the NKVD, Stalin's secret police, were everywhere,
willing to kill anyone even suspected of being a danger to the
Soviet Union.

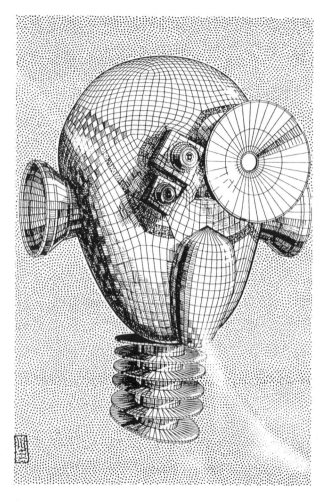

MEDICAL ROBOT. This is a view of the head of a general-purpose medical robot in R. Hunter's time. Robots of this class staffed all of Mojave Center's medical facilities, and performed most medical functions short of major surgery.

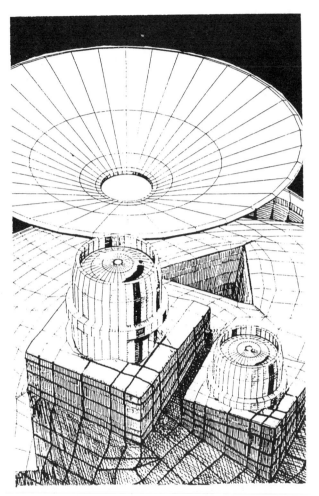

MEDICAL ROBOT CLOSEUP. The diagnostic equipment located on the medical robot's face can identify symptoms of any known human disease. Among other functions, the medical robots diagnostic scanners can scan individual cells for abnormalities.

THE REFUGEE WAREHOUSE. Civilian refugees are crowded into massive empty warehouses after fleeing from the German army. These refugees are in danger from the Soviet secret police as well as the German army.

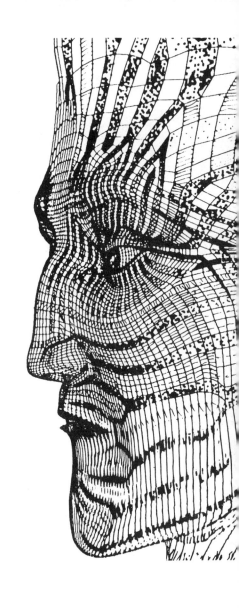

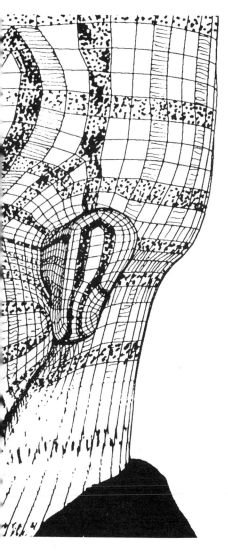

R. HUNTER FACIAL STRUCTURE. Shown here is an analysis of R. Hunter's neural net flow after he has shifted his form to match local environmental conditions.

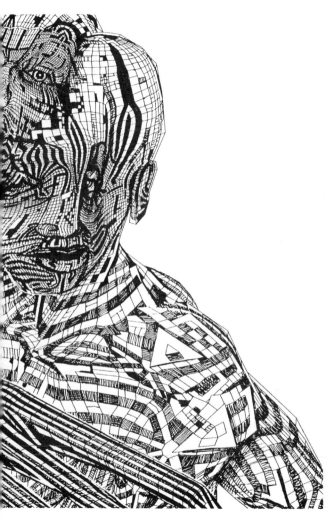

MC ROBOTS MERGED. Three of MC Governor's six independent component robots are shown here. After capturing them in the remote past, R. Hunter merged and deactivated the robots temporarily.

RIDING TO THE FRONT. In the morning, Soviet war refugees are trucked to the outskirts of Moscow to dig miles of trenches in front of the advancing German army. Although the final attack on Moscow never came, the terrified civilians expected it every day.

HUNTER DISGUISED. Here is another of R. Hunter's many disguises. As long as his mass remained constant, R. Hunter could shift his face and surface skin structure in nearly limitless ways.

mans. In this case, we should have plenty of time, since the Soviets so far remain unaware of us."

"Well, we managed with the Germans. I guess we could come up with a better story this time."

"If someone comes to get us, they may wonder where our radio is. Obviously, I cannot reveal that I am a robot with an internal system."

"What do you want to tell them?"

"Since we will have no radio of this era to show them, we must be careful to explain that our radio quit working and was abandoned before they arrived. I recommend that we claim the Germans had us under fire at the time."

"Got it. But isn't that a little premature? First we'd better hope someone shows up at all. Then we can hope they don't demand to see the radio."

"With your agreement, I shall radio for help in Russian to the Red Army."

"Go ahead," Wayne said wryly. "Otherwise, this cold may kill me first."

They stood in silence for a moment, as Ishihara broadcast a message.

"You get anybody?" Wayne asked.

"Not yet."

"What did you say?"

"I was deliberately vague. I said that we were bringing intelligence about the Germans back to the Soviet lines but were stranded."

"Did you send it more than once?"

"Yes, of course. And I shall continue to transmit it at intervals."

"Good."

"But I must question a statement you made a

moment ago about dying of the cold. Before I can allow that to happen, I would have to insist that we leave this time and place."

"Changing to another time has to remain our last resort," said Wayne. "That's a Second Law imperative."

"We discussed this matter in ancient Germany," said Ishihara. "I understand your concern that Hunter will have assigned another robot to apprehend us back in our own time. But of course we do not have to return there. We can jump only a few hours and a few miles if you wish."

"I know," said Wayne. "But if we jump from here to Moscow, for instance, we don't know where we'll appear—maybe right in front of people. And if we move forward at too long an interval, I'm afraid Hunter will already have grabbed MC 4 before we've had a chance."

"I understand," said Ishihara. He hesitated, suddenly moving to face east.

Wayne waited eagerly, sure that he had received something from the Soviets.

"They are coming," said Ishihara.

"How far away are they?"

"I do not know yet. A Red Army unit finally responded to my message on the fourteenth repetition. I said we are civilians escaping from the Germans with military intelligence we wanted to share with the Soviets."

"How were you able to tell them where we are? I have no idea." Wayne looked around in the darkness.

"I could not. I told them I shall transmit to them every minute or so, just counting numbers, so that they can trace the signal as they approach us."

"I hope they hurry. I'm getting colder by the minute."

"They are not far."

"Good," said Wayne. "Do you know what will happen between these two armies here? I mean, I know which side won the war, of course, but what about right here? Do you know anything about that?"

"I have no details."

"None at all?"

"I only know that the Germans will lose this battle outside Moscow," said Ishihara. "They do not take the city, despite what Leutnant Mohr said about it. This is the first Soviet victory of the war."

"Well, let's figure out our story. We want to have it before anyone gets here."

Hunter walked through the dark, nearly deserted streets with his team, pausing to hide in shadows or around corners on the few occasions when they saw a vehicle. They saw no other pedestrians. At the same time, Hunter monitored the radio transmissions in Moscow from the NKVD. The transmissions made reference to a couple of other public buildings that were being used to house displaced citizens.

None of the messages mentioned an exact address. However, Hunter heard references to neighborhoods and streets that helped him choose the team's direction. After nearly an hour of walking through the cold, he approached another warehouse, from which a small amount of light escaped around the edges of a blacked-out window.

"That must be the place," said Hunter. "I can hear the sleeping breaths of many people inside, as Jane suggested earlier."

"What's our story?" Steve moved up next to Hunter, moving slowly with weariness from all the walking. "Won't they want to know what we've been doing out at this hour?"

"As you have occasionally recommended, I shall improvise." Hunter knocked firmly on the front door. "The story we used when we first arrived, without you, should be sufficient."

"What was it?" Steve asked.

Before Hunter could answer, the door opened slightly. A stout, scowling man glared at him. "Yeah, what is it?"

"We are displaced citizens from a farm west of Moscow," said Hunter. "We have fled the Germans and seek shelter for the night."

"The Germans have been at our gates for weeks. Where have you been since then?" The man eyed Steve suspiciously. "Where's he from? He's no Russian."

Steve stepped back.

"My friend is a Mongol who originally came from south of here, down by the Black Sea," Hunter said calmly. "Recently, he worked on the collective farm with us. Here are my sister and my cousin."

"You are a fine, big, strapping fellow," the guard said. "Why aren't you out in the front lines? We have need for men like you."

Hunter patted his left leg. "I can't keep up on the march. Bad leg."

"Oh? And you're out in the cold all night?" The man started to say something else when another man's voice from inside stopped him.

"Let them in, Yevgeny! So you can close the door! You're letting all the cold air inside!"

The first man frowned even more, but he stepped back, holding the door open.

Hunter entered first, judging that more potential danger to his team lay in the uncertainties inside than in the empty street outside. However, this warehouse was little different from the last one. In the weak light from a lamp on the front table, he could see that the warehouse floor was covered with the sleeping people he had first heard a few moments before.

"We have no more blankets." Their host folded his arms across his chest and stared at Hunter. "And we have very little space left."

"It will be fine," Hunter said casually. "Thank you." He led the team down one wall, carefully stepping around or over the people in the way.

As in the other warehouse, people had clustered near the heating vents and had avoided the external walls as much as possible. That once again left some space for the team in one of the back corners. The corner was not exactly warm, but it was much warmer than the streets.

Hunter turned to look at his team members in the shadows and spoke in a whisper. "Is everyone okay?" He glanced past them to see that no one else was listening.

"Yes," whispered Judy. "Good job."

"I'm fine," said Jane.

"Let's get some rest," said Steve.

"Your sleep schedules do not match the time to which we have come," said Hunter. "You will probably not sleep. But we must remain quiet so that we attract no more attention. Your bodies will begin to adjust."

"It's like jet lag," said Steve, with a shrug.

Wayne was shivering uncontrollably out on the steppe by the time headlights appeared in the distance to the east. The lights quivered and jumped as the vehicle rumbled across the frozen steppe toward them. Ishihara waited patiently.

A Soviet armored car finally roared to a stop in front of them. It was designed in a slightly different way from the one Leutnant Mohr had driven, but essentially accomplished the same purpose. The moment it stopped, however, a squad of Soviet soldiers leaped out of the back and fanned out to surround them, aiming their rifles at Wayne and Ishihara. One of them shouted in Russian.

Ishihara raised his hands over his head. Wayne imitated him. Neither of them spoke.

The squad leader shouted again. Two of the soldiers slung their rifles over their shoulders and jogged forward. They frisked Wayne and Ishihara, then stepped back.

The squad leader spoke sharply once more, jerking his head toward the back of the armored car.

"Follow me." Ishihara walked toward it, glancing back at Wayne.

The instruction was unnecessary. Wayne was going to do whatever Ishihara did. They climbed into the back of the armored car, followed by the rest of the squad.

The armored car rumbled forward in a wide turn and drove back in the direction from which it had come. These soldiers were much more alert than the exhausted Germans had been. They kept their weapons trained on the prisoners during the entire ride, and never looked away from them.

Since Ishihara said nothing, Wayne remained silent as well. These Soviet soldiers seemed more dangerous, at least so far, than the Germans ever had. He could only hope that their superiors, like the Germans, would be open to hearing their story. As the icy wind whipped past them, he concentrated on keeping his balance and not making any sudden moves.

The journey did not take very long. The searchlights over Moscow were closer than ever. With the Soviet lines blacked out, however, Wayne suddenly realized that they were coming right up on the lines without any warning. Moscow itself was still some distance away.

The armored car drove through the lines to the rear. When it pulled up in front of a large tent, the squad leader shouted in Russian again. Ishihara jumped to the ground, so Wayne followed him.

Ishihara felt stress under the First Law imperatives. He had to keep Wayne safe or else somehow reach inside his torso cavity quickly and take them both to the safety of another time. His promise to Wayne not to do so unnecessarily, however, prevented him from acting too hastily.

Two men in civilian clothes, wearing long black overcoats and fur hats, came out of the tent. One of the civilians conferred briefly with the squad leader in Russian. The other soldiers still held their weapons trained on Wayne and Ishihara.

"This way," said the civilian to Ishihara in Russian, nodding toward the tent.

Turning, Ishihara led Wayne into the tent. Ishihara was surprised that civilians were going to talk to them. Here in military lines, he had expected to be grilled by military officers again.

Only a battered wooden table and a couple of

wooden stools stood inside the tent. The dirty canvas walls protected them from the wind but did little else. One of the civilians spoke in a coldly formal tone.

"What nationality are you?"

"My friend is Swedish and I am Swiss."

They had agreed upon this story while waiting out on the steppe. The Soviets would not like to hear that Ishihara had any connection to Japan because of their historical resentment; in 1905, the Japanese had defeated Czarist Russia in war. If Wayne and Ishihara were both Swedish, however, their hosts would expect them to communicate in that language. Since Ishihara knew that Switzerland had also been neutral in this war, claiming to be Swiss would explain their language differences.

"My friend does not speak Russian or any of the languages spoken in Switzerland and I do not speak Swedish," said Ishihara. "Therefore, we speak English to each other and I can translate Russian for him."

"Very well."

Ishihara turned to Wayne and explained this exchange in English.

"All right," said Wayne. "Any idea who these guys are? They aren't officers."

"I am not certain." Ishihara turned. "Who are you? What are your names?"

"You don't need to know."

Ishihara translated this, as well.

Wayne nodded. Then he waited, as one of the two civilians asked questions. His partner remained silent.

Ishihara prepared to translate throughout the conversation.

"What are your names?" The man in charge, a stout, frowning man, looked back and forth between them from under bushy eyebrows.

"Wayne Nystrom and R. Ishihara."

"What are you doing here? What is your purpose?"

"We are pro-Soviet agents from neutral countries," said Ishihara, matching their host's formal tone. "For many months, we have been pursuing a German agent across much of central and eastern Europe."

"Why are you wearing those ridiculous clothes?"

"We were given these clothes while crossing the mountains fleeing the enemy."

The man studied them both for a moment. "You say you are chasing a German agent?"

"Two agents," said Wayne. "Remember Hunter."

"Oh, yes."

"Eh? You aren't certain of your mission?" The Russian glowered at them both suspiciously. "You are changing your story, now?"

"Our first mission is to apprehend a man code-named MC 4," said Ishihara.

"However, another German agent is hoping to warn him about us first," said Wayne. "His name is Hunter. Naturally, we must stop him, too."

"This agent who is code-named MC 4," said the Russian, still eyeing Ishihara closely. "Do you know what his name is? Or what name he is using?"

"No," said Ishihara.

"What is his mission in Moscow?"

Ishihara was aware that Wayne was deliberately remaining quiet, letting Ishihara take the lead. If they both answered simultaneously, and contradicted each other, they would lose their credibility completely. Wayne watched Ishihara.

"We believe that MC 4 will observe Red Army military placements," said Ishihara.

"Then he will not enter the city proper?"

"We expect that he will also infiltrate the city to gain further information. Then he will radio what he learns back to German lines."

"If he has preceded you here, he may already have radioed this information." Their host turned to Wayne. "You have said very little. Do you think you are too late?"

"Uh—no," said Wayne slowly, as Ishihara continued to translate. "We aren't too late. I don't think he can risk too many radio transmissions from here to the German lines."

"He can't risk too many? What do you mean?" For the first time, the Russian sounded less hostile.

"Well, if he radios back too soon, he runs the risk of being caught before he has learned everything he can," said Wayne. "He won't want to take that chance."

"Then what do you expect him to do?"

"I think he'll probably try to look around the Red Army positions first, then enter the city before he transmits anything."

"Yes," said Ishihara, nodding quickly. "This would match his pattern of behavior in the past."

"Eh? What pattern do you mean?"

"He will try to gather all his information first and then transmit it at once. A single radio transmission will lower the risk to himself."

"That's right," Wayne said quickly. "That's what I was trying to say."

"Now what about this other agent? Is 'Hunter' his code name or the one he is giving to others?"

"This is what he calls himself," said Wayne. "We, uh, don't know what his code name is."

"What do they look like?"

The second Russian took out a pad of paper and a pencil from his overcoat and prepared to take notes.

"They are opposites," said Wayne. "MC 4 is a short, slender man, very slight and quick."

"Hunter is tall and brawny," said Ishihara. "Blond hair, blue eyes."

The man taking notes nodded as he scribbled. When he had caught up with what they had said already, Wayne and Ishihara finished giving him descriptions of the two robots. Wayne had decided that MC 4 and Hunter, being robots, could adequately take care of themselves.

However, Wayne did not want to be responsible for the human members of Hunter's team falling into the hands of the Soviet government. He did not mention them. When Ishihara also avoided giving any information about them, Wayne decided that the First Law prohibited Ishihara from doing so.

Wayne hoped merely to cause delays for Hunter. If Hunter got into real trouble, of course, he could ultimately take his team out of danger by returning to their own time. Meanwhile, maybe the Soviet authorities could somehow help Wayne and Ishihara locate MC 4.

On the other hand, the authorities might want to keep these spies for themselves if they caught them.

"Both these agents are clever," said Wayne. He was not sure what he was going to say, but he wanted to convince their hosts that these two fugitives should be brought to Wayne and Ishihara. "To get the most out of them, we should participate in the questioning."

"Yes, of course," said the first man.

"Only we two can fully interpret their answers and their information," Ishihara added, apparently picking up Wayne's concern.

"We must ask them about their activities on earlier missions, as well," said Wayne.

"What about the German lines?" The second man, who had been silent to this point, finally spoke. "What have you observed that can be of use to us?"

Wayne hesitated. Ishihara saw that he did not want to pass information that could somehow alter history in a significant way. He needed prodding.

Ishihara gave Wayne a very subtle nod of encouragement. "I am certain we shall win," said Ishihara. "The upcoming battle will be a victory."

"Yes? Why are you so sure?" The civilian's tone was a little more open now.

"What is your name?" Ishihara asked. "So we can all become acquainted."

"I am Agent Raskov," said the second man.

The first man, who had refused to introduce them earlier, scowled in resignation. "I am Agent Konev."

"Why are you so certain that we will win the next battle?" Agent Raskov asked again.

"The German army is dying on its feet," said Wayne. "They are cold. In fact, their soldiers don't even have winter clothes to wear."

"Eh?" Agent Raskov glanced in surprise at his partner. "How can this be?"

"Their generals were overconfident," said Ishihara. "They expected to have taken Moscow before winter began. Already, the Red Army has stalled their plans."

"So they are cold." Agent Raskov turned back to Wayne. "What else?"

"Their morale is low. They are totally dispirited. They really just want to go home."

"They do?" Agent Konev raised his bushy eyebrows. "Are they ripe for subversion?"

"Uh . . ." Wayne glanced uncertainly at Ishihara. "What do you think?"

"No," said Ishihara. "The German soldiers are discouraged but they are not cowards or traitors."

"Maybe they fear Hitler more than they fear us," said Agent Konev.

"Yes, that is possible."

"We were in Panzer Group 3," said Ishihara. "I can tell you its placement."

"Excellent." Agent Raskov turned a page in his notebook. "Go ahead."

Wayne waited patiently while Ishihara described German placements. He was certain that these were not secrets; the Soviets already knew where the Germans had been. Finally, when Ishihara had finished, their hosts seemed to soften a little. Agent Raskov even smiled very slightly as he put away his notebook.

"Your information about the placement of the enemy matches our own," said Agent Raskov.

"Why was no previous liaison made with us?" Agent Konev shook his head.

"Yes, we should have heard from you," said Agent Raskov. "That is true."

"We apologize," said Ishihara, with a faint shrug.

Agent Konev turned to Wayne. He acted more relaxed now, though he remained reserved. "Since you are traveling without credentials, you should have given us some form of advance notice."

"We would have if it had been possible," said Wayne. "We were afraid that the Germans would intercept any radio communication we made too soon."

"That was a real danger," said Agent Raskov. "You seem to have handled it well."

"By the time we did radio you, we were closer to Red Army lines than German lines, so we felt it was safe enough to attempt," said Wayne.

"We took a considerable risk contacting you when we did," said Ishihara.

"How did you get across the no-man's-land?" Agent Raskov asked. "I mean to say, as far across it as you got?"

"It was a long, cold walk," said Ishihara. "And we only dared use our radio when we realized that we could not make the trip on our own."

"And where is your radio now?" Agent Konev asked. "Do the soldiers have it?"

"No," said Ishihara. "It malfunctioned. Since it was heavy, we abandoned it under fire from the Germans as we fled."

Both Russians nodded.

Ishihara did not know if their hosts completely believed their story. However, he could see that they, like the Germans, were at least undecided about them. He was certain that the fact that he had taken the initiative to contact them lent some positive weight to their story, too.

"What help can you give us?" Ishihara asked. "In our search for the two enemy agents?"

"We must confer further on this," said Agent Raskov. "However, first we can give you some hot coffee." He grinned openly for the first time. "Coffee is rare these days, carefully rationed. But we can offer you some."

"I could use something to eat, too, if that's possible," said Wayne.

"Of course." Agent Raskov glanced at his watch. "We can arrange it. As for the help, however, it is quite late. What help do you want?"

"Where would two strangers find shelter in Moscow?" Ishihara asked. "Traveling individually, with no one to help them, where would they go?"

"Public housing," said Agent Konev.

"That's right," said Agent Raskov. "It would be easier for them now, in wartime, than in peacetime. So many people have been displaced by the war."

"Then we would like to visit these places," said Ishihara. "To look for our quarry."

Agent Raskov looked at his partner. "I think we can do this tonight."

"Yes. Tonight is good. If we find these enemy infiltrators while they are sleeping, they will be easier to identify and apprehend."

"I agree," said Agent Raskov. "First we will feed you. Then we will drive you into the city and see if we can take care of this matter."

"Thank you." Wayne relaxed a little. Hot coffee, food, and help finding MC 4 were the best news they had received since arriving in this time. "Can you find us ordinary clothes?"

"Wait here," said Agent Raskov. "We will send someone with coffee and something for you to eat. If we can find clothes, we shall bring them."

"Thank you," said Wayne.

The two agents left the tent without saying anything else. In only a few moments, they were out of human hearing. However, Ishihara heard them still talking to each other with his enhanced hearing.

"How much time should we spend looking for these other agents?" Agent Raskov asked quietly.

"We should look tonight, at least, in case we can find them quickly," said Agent Konev.

"And then?"

"We must have more information about our two guests. At dawn, we must interrogate them thoroughly. We cannot allow ourselves to work with only partial information."

"Even if we find these two agents? That would back up their story."

"No matter what we find," said Agent Konev. "Their story is too thin and they have no documents to back it up. We must interrogate them as we would an enemy."

Hunter lay motionless in the darkened warehouse. He had not shut himself down, but was conserving energy by not moving. Of course, he pretended to sleep at the same time. When a firm, resounding knock sounded at the main door, he did not move, but instantly magnified his hearing. He checked his internal clock and found that the time was 3:17 A.M.

The knocking was repeated, loudly, as someone from the front went to answer it.

"Who's there?" One of the guards spoke cautiously from inside the door.

"Agents Raskov and Konev, NKVD."

As the door was opened, Hunter reached out and gently woke Steve.

"Steve, can you hear me?" Hunter whispered.

"Yeah."

"I believe the NKVD is looking for Judy. You and Jane move closer to her. Cover her face with something. I will try to create a diversion."

"What?" Steve opened his eyes, startled. "The NKVD is here after all?"

Hunter slipped his belt unit into Steve's hand. He knew Steve would not leave for their own time without him except in an extreme emergency. "I have already set the controls. Use it if you must."

Steve nodded and moved over to wake up Jane and Judy, whispering to them quietly.

Hunter listened to the two NKVD agents ask the guards about Hunter by both his name and his description. The overhead lights came on, causing a number of people in the crowd to stir. Hunter looked up and saw one of the guards pointing directly toward this corner.

The two agents began working their way down the length of the warehouse. Their way was blocked by all the sleeping and newly awakened people on the floor. Hunter had a few seconds to consider what to do.

He was puzzled by their possessing his description but not Judy's. Still, he expected that these agents would take the entire team if they found the group together. He had to separate himself from the others immediately.

Hunter did not want to return his entire team to their own time in front of so many witnesses. Two such events would definitely be discussed and would influence the local authorities in some way. Having everyone flee out the rear door again might not be as effective this time; the NKVD agents would maintain pursuit, where as the ordinary guards in the previous warehouse had not bothered.

The two agents stared at Hunter with grim determination as they stumbled through the crowd.

To prevent them from taking the human members of his team, Hunter could allow himself to be taken. He felt he could manage to get away later if they arrested him. His team members would still be in some danger without him, but totally avoiding significant risk was now impossible.

To help the rest of his team escape, he would have to lead the NKVD agents away from them.

Hunter got to his feet suddenly. The two agents

both stopped in surprise, looking up at him; maybe his height startled them. Instead of running, however, Hunter strode toward them, imitating the scowls on both their faces.

The two Russians recovered from their surprise. "Stop, comrade," said one. "I am Agent Raskov. You must come with us."

Since Hunter wanted to keep their attention on him, he did not bother to answer. He suddenly darted to his right, stepping over a sleepy, puzzled elderly man. As the two agents moved to block his way, he jumped over someone else to a small open spot on the floor.

"Halt! I command you!"

More people were sitting up, blinking in the light and looking around.

Hunter, of course, could have easily leaped through the crowd, throwing the two agents aside with his greater strength. Instead, he was hoping to make them work to capture him, so that they would forget about arresting his team members. He hesitated, giving the agents a chance to maneuver closer.

"You will not be hurt, comrade," said Agent Konev, as he came forward, pulling a handgun out of his overcoat. "Not unless you force us to get angry."

Around him, those who were awake gasped and squealed in sudden fear. Some scuttled away from him, still on the floor. Others lay flat, their eyes wide.

Hunter had been prepared to move toward the front door again. Now he stopped, staring at the gun aimed at him. He wondered if these agents would actually risk opening fire in the crowded room. From what Judy had said about this society, he estimated that they would.

The Third Law prevented him from taking an unnecessary risk to himself, of course, but the First Law completely prevented him from fleeing now, for fear that bystanders would be shot by mistake. He raised his hands slowly and did not move. The other agent also drew a gun.

"Do not fire," said Hunter. "Do not endanger anyone else here."

"Turn around," said Agent Raskov.

"Agreed. Please do not fire." Hunter obeyed. He felt himself being frisked. With the demands of the First Law dominating his thoughts, he fully expected that they would next go after the humans on his team—probably forcing Steve to take them all back to their own time.

Instead, to his surprise, each agent took one of his arms and they walked him forward through the warehouse.

Ishihara and Wayne had been left out in the backseat of the car each time that Raskov and Konev went inside another building. Their hosts had found them each a long, black woolen overcoat, but no other clothes to wear. Wayne kept his cloak bundled carefully under his arm.

For almost two hours after reaching Moscow, they had gone to one facility after another, looking for MC 4 and Hunter among the people displaced by the war. Ishihara had already told Wayne what he had overheard with his enhanced hearing about Raskov and Konev interrogating them when morning arrived, whether or not they located the two enemy agents tonight.

Ishihara knew that the interrogation would involve torture. Under the First Law, he could not allow Wayne to take that risk of harm. They had to escape sometime tonight.

"When are we going to make our move?" Wayne asked. "Wouldn't this be a good time to get away from them? We're just sitting here."

"I fear that simply jumping out of the car and running would put you in danger of freezing to death, without improving our chances of avoiding recapture."

"Yeah. Well . . . if we don't escape to begin with, we won't have to worry about being recaptured at all." Wayne sighed. "I don't want to freeze out there, either, but if we're going to go, shouldn't we just do it?"

"Yes, you have a point."

"Hey—they've taken a lot longer in this one than the others. Before, they just talked to a few people at the door, got the lights turned on, and came back out. You think that means something?"

Ishihara turned up his hearing to maximum. Suddenly he recognized Hunter's voice telling someone not "to fire." Ishihara knew a weapon was being held on him.

"Get in the driver's seat," Ishihara said suddenly, opening his own door. "Now, quickly!" He got out and closed the door as quietly as he could.

Wayne climbed over the front seat and rolled down the window so he could speak to Ishihara. "But now what? I don't know how to work this thing."

Ishihara ran around to the driver's side "They are bringing Hunter out. We must avoid him for the good of your own mission."

"Okay! But what do I *do*?"

Ishihara leaned inside, pointing. "Push down that pedal, the clutch, with your left foot. Hold on to the steering wheel." He grabbed the gearshift and moved it. "Hold this right here and, let up with your left foot."

"Got it." Wayne did as he was told. "How do you know how to work this thing?"

"I observed the driver carefully as we were riding before, and listened to the engine and gear sounds."

"But he used a key to turn it on, didn't he? And he must have taken it with him. It's not here."

"I realized that this vehicle is one I have some knowledge about. It will start a couple of other ways than by normal use of the key."

"It will?"

"Use your other foot on the other two pedals. Those are the brake and accelerator."

"All right. That's the same as in our electric vehicles back home."

Ishihara hurried to the rear of the car. His hearing revealed three sets of footsteps inside the warehouse walking resolutely toward the front door. Hoping that his information about this car was reliable, he leaned against the back of the car and used all of his strength to push it. Slowly, the car rolled forward.

The vehicle was on a fairly level stretch of pavement. In a moment, Ishihara had it moving faster. Suddenly the car jerked a couple of times and the engine made a coughing noise. Finally it roared to life.

"Halt! I order you to stop!" Agent Konev's voice came from the front door.

Ishihara ran around the right side of the moving car. He yanked the passenger door open and jumped inside. Then he slammed it shut.

"Now what?" Wayne asked frantically, pushing the accelerator to the floor. "It won't go very fast!"

"Push down the clutch." Ishihara reached over at the same time and put his hand over Wayne's on the gearshift, moving it for him. The engine roared and jerked; then the car sped up as it moved into second gear.

"Halt!" A gunshot followed the shout.

Wayne yanked the steering wheel to turn a corner, making the tires squeal.

Ishihara turned to look behind them just before they completed the turn. In the shadows, Agent Raskov held his gun pointing into the air. Next to him, Agent Konev was holding Hunter by one arm.

"Now what do I do?" Wayne shouted over the roar of the engine as he gripped the steering wheel. "This can't be right! It's going a little faster, but it doesn't sound like it did before!" He was driving down a city street now, but much too slowly.

"Push down the clutch again." As before, Ishihara grabbed his hand over the gearshift and moved it into third gear. Instantly, the engine noise lowered and the car sped up.

"Okay," Wayne muttered. "I'm getting some idea about how this works now. But where am I going?"

Ishihara pointed into the shadows ahead. "Turn left at the next corner."

Wayne turned too fast. The tires squealed again and they both were thrown to the right in their seats. He hit the brake and slowed down, belatedly.

"Uh, sorry," said Wayne. "I'll need a lot of practice to get this right." As soon as he had the steering under control again, he pressed the accelerator and sped up.

"Right now, we need to use an evasive pattern," said Ishihara. "Our hosts are probably telephoning their main office for help right away."

"Yeah? What are we going to do, then?"

"Once we have put some distance behind us, we can plan where to go. At the moment, however, I suggest you slow down. We do not want to attract attention by going unusually fast."

"Oh. Yeah, I guess not." Wayne carefully braked slightly. This time the car slowed down smoothly. "There. That wasn't too bad."

Ishihara looked around. The streets of Moscow were empty and scoured by the wintry winds. So far, he could see no one following them.

"I am not certain what to recommend now," said Ishihara. "The NKVD at large, of course, will have the description and license number of this car as soon as the agents call in a report."

"Oh, yeah," said Wayne. "Shouldn't we stop somewhere and leave it behind, then?"

"We can risk using it for a short time. Then, as you say, we must find a place to hide the car. We shall have to flee on foot again after that."

"Okay," said Wayne. He clenched the steering wheel hard in both hands, tense with his crash course in learning to drive this vintage vehicle. "Just tell me what to do."

Steve remained flat on the floor of the warehouse as Hunter toyed with the NKVD agents. When the agents took Hunter out, Steve cautiously sat up. Then Jane and Judy pushed themselves up, too, and looked around.

Most of the weary Russians around them lay

back down again to go back to sleep. Some whispered fearfully to each other. A few people lined up for the rest room.

"They're used to it," Judy whispered. "That's the worst part of it."

"Is that why they're just going back to sleep?" Jane asked, looking around.

"Yes," said Judy. "Everyone has become so used to this sort of treatment that they just hope no one is coming for them or their loved ones."

"That's horrible," said Steve.

"Yes, it certainly is. And beyond their own personal safety, the oppression doesn't matter that much to them anymore. After the back-breaking work they do all day, going back to sleep is enough."

"I thought they'd come for us, too," said Judy. "This doesn't make any sense. The guards at the front must have told them we came in together."

"I don't get it, either." Steve patted the bulge made by the belt device inside his shirt to make sure it was secure. "I'm using the latrine. Be right back."

He got to his feet and joined the line at the rest room. While he waited there, he kept one arm over the bulge in his shirt to hide it. Before his turn came, the people at the front table turned off the overhead lights, leaving on only a small lamp at their table. Steve relaxed a little, knowing that no one could any longer see him clearly in the shadows.

When Steve finally got inside, he turned on his lapel pin and began whispering. "Hunter, Steve here."

"Yes, Steve."

"What can you tell me? What's going on?"

"I know very little. At the moment, the agents who arrested me are escorting me down the street on foot. Clearly, they had not come for Judy after all."

"Why didn't they take all of us?"

"They only gave my name and description to the guards. The guards merely pointed me out. No one told them that the rest of you were with me."

"How did they get your description?"

"I believe Wayne Nystrom and R. Ishihara gave it to them."

"Huh? How do you know that?"

"The agents' car was stolen just as we left the warehouse. From my glimpse of the thieves in the shadows, I am certain that R. Ishihara and Wayne Nystrom took the car."

"What do you want me to do?" Steve asked. "While you're alone with those guys, you could get away and meet us somewhere. Should we slip out the back door again?"

"No," Hunter said firmly. "I do not want the team on the run in the cold again. Remain sheltered there for the night. For now, remain calm and patient. I shall not risk calling you, so call me when you can."

"All right."

"Be warned that I may have to change my appearance before I return."

"Okay."

"Hunter out."

Steve worked his way back to Jane and Judy in the dimly lighted room and sat down. No one else was moving around now. He relayed the conversation with Hunter to them in a whisper.

"I guess Hunter's right," Judy whispered back. "We can't do much to help him anyway."

Steve nodded. "I guess."

"Definitely," said Judy. "Besides, how could we agree on a place to meet? We don't know the city."

"That's true," said Jane. "And Hunter has so many more abilities than we have. He has a lot more flexibility without us. He won't have to worry about us this way, since we're sheltered here."

"All right, all right," said Steve. "Suppose we focus on our main target, instead. We're spending all our time just trying to get along here. But what about MC 4?"

"I've been thinking about him," said Judy. "Originally, I believed that the First Law would induce MC 4 to interfere with the German advance."

"I remember," said Jane.

"Well, maybe I was off base about that," Judy said slowly. "Actually, as I recall, the German military is in very poor shape right now."

"They're the real aggressors, though, aren't they?" Steve asked.

"Well, yes," said Judy. "They *are* the aggressors, in that they're standing on Soviet territory and they've been marching on Moscow. But in the coming battle, the Soviets actually conduct a counterattack."

"I get it," said Jane. "So now you think MC 4 might try to prevent violence by interfering with the Soviet counterattack."

"Well, it's just one idea. But also, MC 4 may learn about the NKVD itself. Their political prisoners are tortured and sent to labor camps where they are worked to death. MC 4 could be drawn to protect the labor camp prisoners from harm."

"I can see that possibility, too," said Jane. "Do you have others?"

"Two more. The Soviet army's German prisoners of war are also treated brutally. Over on the German side, Soviet prisoners die by the thousands."

"Labor camp prisoners and prisoners of war on both sides," said Steve. "Plus the Soviet army command. That's at least three important places MC 4 might pick out—not to mention any specific situations he happens to see."

"I haven't narrowed the possibilities very much, I'm afraid," said Judy.

Jane nodded. "So many humans are being harmed in so many ways near here right now that the First Law might draw MC 4 in almost any direction. And, of course, he will have to begin by putting his energy into learning all of this. Maybe we're getting ahead of ourselves. He could just be trying to find clothing and a way to fit in at this stage."

"All right," said Steve. "I know our sleep schedules aren't in line with this time zone, but we might as well lie down and relax a little. When morning comes, we'll see if we can meet Hunter somewhere and plan something."

"Good idea," said Jane.

Steve sighed. He was concerned about Hunter, but could not see anything he could do at the moment. This society was much more structured, even in the disruption of wartime, than the earlier ones the team had visited. Operating in it would be much more complicated than he had realized.

A pounding knock on the front door startled him. Feeling a surge of adrenaline, he forced himself to remain prone and simply turned to look toward the front. As one of the guards spoke through the door and then opened it, the thumping continued. People sleeping inside began to stir.

Four men in long, black coats strode inside. One of them switched on the lights. They had the same manner and clothing as the NKVD agents Steve had seen before.

"Everyone up! Immediately! Wake up! Stand against the wall!" The first man barked the orders. He drew a handgun and held it without pointing it at anyone in particular.

Two of his companions began grabbing people's arms and pulling them to their feet. Most of the people were groggy from sleep and confused. The fourth man glanced around and then walked over to the front table, where he started looking around carefully.

Steve pushed himself up and helped pull Jane and Judy to their feet. At least the three of them were already awake. He led them over to the wall where the others were being herded, so they could get lost in the crowd.

The agent holding the gun kept it on the crowd. The man who had begun inspecting the front table slowly worked his way through storage cabinets down the wall toward the rest room, pulling out whatever he found and letting it fall. The last two men began kicking apart the bedding and personal items on the floor.

Since they had asked no questions, Steve could not tell right away what they were looking for. He watched as the two agents in the middle of the floor shook everything apart, throwing belongings in all directions. The people huddled around them watched in terror, without protesting.

"Does this happen often?" Steve whispered to Judy, lowering his head to stay out of sight.

"As often as they want," said Judy. "But they're looking for something specific, I think."

Jane nodded. "Something too big for people to hide on their bodies. That's why they aren't searching anybody."

No one else spoke as the three men systematically tore apart all of the personal belongings and threw the items in the storage cabinets onto the floor. The man searching the far wall also inspected the rest room. Finally, after they had finished, they turned and faced the crowd.

"Two secret radio transmitters have been detected functioning in this neighborhood," said the man with the gun. "Who knows something about them?"

Steve froze with tension. His call to Hunter, when Hunter had still been nearby outside, had been picked up by Soviet receivers, along with Hunter's response. For the authorities to have estimated the location of the two sources, at least two receivers had to have overheard them, and probably more. Since the man had used the word "neighborhood," they had not been able to focus specifically on this building. Obviously, however, they had come very close.

Steve chastised himself for being careless. In all of their previous missions, radio had been unknown and, therefore, completely secret. Their only worry had been to avoid having Hunter call them on their lapel pins while they were in the hearing of local people.

He had completely forgotten that their messages could be intercepted by local authorities. Since Hunter had not warned him of this at the time, even Hunter might have taken the possibility lightly. Now they had caused this disruption and potential danger to everyone in the warehouse.

The crowd remained silent, some eyeing the four NKVD agents with fear and others turning their faces away. In turn, the four men stared at individuals in the crowd, frowning with suspicion. No one spoke for a long moment.

Steve frantically tried to remember the content of his conversation with Hunter. He remembered that Judy's first name had been mentioned and also the names of Wayne Nystrom and Ishihara. He had addressed Hunter by name and used his own first name—and they had spoken in English. That alone would mark them as foreigners. Also, the brief exchange had raised the possibility of sneaking out to meet, which certainly would have sounded suspicious. Beyond that, however, he could not recall the exact wording of the discussion.

The agent with the gun walked up to the crowd and spoke in a low voice to someone in the crowd. Steve could not see him. He could not make out the words, either, but the tone was menacing, aimed at intimidation.

Steve decided that radio meant something much more important here than it did in his own time. Though his knowledge of history did not come close to that of Hunter or Judy, and was not as good as even Jane's, he supposed that radio was the only broadcast tool available in this time. It would be especially useful for intelligence agents. These NKVD agents were probably looking for spies, though they had no idea that a transmitter and receiver could be small enough to hide in a lapel pin.

The agent with the gun shoved the person he had been talking to out of the way and studied the crowd, looking for someone else to question.

Wayne concentrated so hard on driving the car without running up on the sidewalk that he had no time to be scared. He turned corners when Ishihara suggested he do so, and could slow down enough not to make the tires squeal. However, Ishihara still had to tell him when to shift gears and to help him move the gearshift while he depressed the clutch. If Ishihara did not tell him to turn, Wayne simply drove straight down the dark streets.

"I am surprised," said Ishihara. "I have continued to monitor NKVD radio traffic. No alert has gone out for the NKVD to search for this car."

"No alert has gone out? Why not?"

"I can only conclude that agents Konev and Raskov have not yet reported that we stole their car."

"Really? They've had plenty of time."

"I would have thought so."

Wayne grinned. "Of course, their radio is in this car. I guess they'd have to look for a phone."

"Yes," said Ishihara. "This means we are free to

keep this car for now. We are in no danger of a specific search by the NKVD at large until they report its theft."

"Well, that's good. At least the heater works." Wayne thought a moment. "But *why* haven't those two agents reported that we took their car?"

"I do not know. Perhaps they have had difficulty locating a telephone."

"Don't they have a lot of authority, though? They could just commandeer a phone, couldn't they?"

"Maybe at this hour, they have literally not found one available."

"Can't they just pound on someone's door to get a phone if they really want to? The way they knocked on those doors to the public housing in the middle of the night?"

"I believe you are correct, to the limit of my knowledge," said Ishihara.

"So why haven't they reported in?"

"I do not know," said Ishihara. "We could turn on the receiver in this car for you to hear, if you understood Russian."

"I wish I did." The mystery made Wayne uncomfortable, even though it seemed to be to their advantage at the moment. "Well, where are we going?"

"We must find you shelter for the night," said Ishihara. "It has been a long night so far. We cannot risk your sleeping in this vehicle, for fear the report will be made and the search will begin."

"Is there anything we can do about finding MC 4? While we still have this car?"

"My only suggestion is that we search through

crowds, especially where a First Law imperative might draw MC 4 to take action."

"I guess that won't apply in the middle of the night when the city's asleep."

"I estimate you are correct."

"Okay." Wayne shrugged. "So, what should we do to find shelter, then?"

"A couple of blocks from where we took the car, I saw another large building that may house displaced citizens. My hearing told me that many people were sleeping inside. I shall direct you back there and we shall go to the door."

"I'm ready when you are."

Wayne drove according to Ishihara's directions. They slowly made their way back to the neighborhood where they had begun. As Wayne recognized one of the blocks, he started looking for pedestrians.

"What if they're still here? Hunter and those agents? We don't want them to see us again."

"I have been looking for any sign of them. I have not seen any. The warehouse from which we took the car is still out of sight."

"How close to it are we going to get?"

"No closer than this. Turn left in the alley just ahead of us and stop the car at the right curb."

"All right."

Wayne turned left and braked nearly to a stop. The car jerked to a sudden halt and the engine died. He shrugged at Ishihara. "Sorry."

"I should have told you to depress the clutch as we stopped," said Ishihara. "Never mind that now. We will get out and knock on the door."

Wayne grabbed his bundled cloak and followed

Ishihara around the corner. At least their overcoats hid their tunics and leggings. They approached a very large building, barely visible in the faint moonlight. Ishihara led him to the front door and knocked.

At first nothing happened. Ishihara knocked several more times. Finally, Wayne heard foot-steps and the door creaked open slightly. An elderly woman with long white hair falling about her shoulders looked out.

"Please, comrade," said Ishihara. "We have been turned away from many places tonight. We only need a small space in which to sleep."

Yawning, the woman glanced at both of them. Then she nodded. She stepped back and opened the door.

Wayne followed Ishihara inside, relieved to feel the warmth. The woman switched on a small lamp. In the light it threw, Wayne could see that sleeping people filled the floor. A few lying within the range of the lamp stirred slightly; otherwise, the light did not disturb anyone.

The woman gestured vaguely toward the room at large; apparently she was telling them to find their own places. Then she stood next to the lamp, waiting for them to do so before turning it off again. Ishihara found a small spot for them along one wall. They sat down there, and Wayne rolled up in his cloak. A moment later, the woman turned out the light.

Hunter's glimpse of Wayne and Ishihara had been brief and limited by the shadows, but it had been enough to identify them. The agents

who had just taken him into custody had been
furious. While one held Hunter's arm, the other had shouted in rage, stomping his feet and
firing a warning shot into the air after the
departing vehicle. During that same few seconds,
Steve had radioed Hunter from just inside the
building.

As the two agents had argued with each other,
Hunter had overheard their names. Agent Raskov,
the angrier one, had wanted to go back inside
and use the warehouse telephone to report the
theft of the car. However, Agent Konev had absolutely forbade it on the grounds that they would
look bad, even incompetent, to the people inside.
Hunter observed that Agent Konev was the senior partner, with the authority to make the final
decision.

Since that argument, the two agents had been
marching Hunter up the street between them.
Each one held one of his arms and walked in
silence. Hunter was not certain if they had a clear
plan themselves. He did understand Agent Konev's
position, however. When a government functioned
by terrorizing its own citizens, its agents could
only lose power by revealing their personal fal-
libility.

At any time, of course, Hunter could pull away
from them by brute force. He did not want to
do that except in an emergency. If possible, he
wanted to satisfy the NKVD agents that he was
no threat and depart from them on good terms.
Otherwise, the team would remain fugitives from
the NKVD for the rest of their time here. That
could only damage their chances of finding MC 4.

"All right, hold it." Agent Raskov brought them to a stop. "Are we going to walk all night? Even if we don't report to the head office that the car was stolen, surely we can call someone for help."

"Who?" Agent Konev demanded gruffly. "How many of our fellow agents want to see us reassigned, so they could move up into our places? All they need is something to use against us. We don't dare turn to any of them."

"Not every colleague wants our jobs. What about the two guys you worked with last year?"

"Hah! They would love to see us both in Siberian labor camps, comrade."

"Well, even if we walk all the way to the office, someone will notice our car is not there—in the morning, after daylight." Agent Raskov sighed. "I'm very tired."

"You may interrogate me here," said Hunter. "If it would be more convenient."

"Shut up," said Agent Konev.

Hunter saw that he was not particularly angry. Since Hunter had been docile to this point, and both agents had handguns, he had not challenged their control of the situation. He decided to risk speaking again.

"Why did you take me?"

"I just told you—" Agent Konev started.

"Don't waste your breath on him," Agent Raskov interrupted. "What are we going to do?"

"Have you been influenced by Wayne Nystrom and Mr. Ishihara?" Hunter spoke in a calm, unemotional tone. He had no idea, of course, if they had given their right names.

Both men turned to him in surprise.

"What have they told you?" Hunter asked.

"Shut up," Agent Konev repeated. He was still studying Hunter's face, however, with new interest.

"You know them personally?" Agent Raskov asked.

"Yes, I do," said Hunter. "I suspect they are using you for their own ends."

"What does that mean?" Agent Konev demanded.

"I think it's obvious," said Agent Raskov. "We've been duped, comrade. They sent us on a diversionary chase and stole our vehicle. Maybe Hunter, here, is not at all that they claimed he was."

"Well, maybe he is. We certainly can't afford to make another blunder tonight."

"Granted," said Agent Raskov. "Let's go into an apartment building and start knocking on doors. Sooner or later, we'll find someone who has a telephone. We don't have to give any explanations about our car."

"All right," Agent Konev said wearily. "We must get to work on this. I agree."

Hunter patiently allowed them to take him wherever they wished. They marched him to the front of a darkened apartment building, where Agent Raskov remained out on the sidewalk with him. Agent Konev pounded on the locked front door, waited, and then hammered on it again. The sound was loud on the quiet street. Finally someone opened it. Agent Konev identified himself and was allowed inside.

Hunter waited only six minutes with Agent Raskov before Agent Konev came back out of the building.

"Did you find a phone?" Agent Raskov asked.

"Yes." Agent Konev nodded grimly. "I did not explain, not yet."

"We will have to explain soon. Who else was on duty? Who is coming to get us, comrade?"

"The night clerk is driving out."

"Oh, young Mikhail? At least he will keep his mouth shut." Agent Raskov let out a long sigh.

"Yes, he will."

They waited out on the street for only about ten minutes before a car drew up to the curb. Hunter allowed himself to be directed into the backseat between the two agents. No one spoke as they rode away.

The car parked behind a large building. Hunter recognized it as the same one from which he had rescued Judy. He was taken into an unmarked back door. Inside, he found himself at the opposite end of the same hallway where he had bluffed his way in to get Judy.

For a few minutes, the agents locked him up alone in an interrogation room. It was similar to the one in which Judy had been held, with a table, a single lamp, and several chairs. The walls had no windows. A steam radiator against one wall provided some heat. He sat down in a chair.

When the door opened, his two hosts came in, now without their overcoats, and shut it. They sat down across the table from him, studying him grimly. He waited for them to speak.

"Who are you, Hunter? Where did you come from?" Agent Konev looked him in the eye.

"I was a farm worker west of Moscow until the Germans came. Then I fled into the city with everyone else." By now, using their own speech as a model, Hunter had polished and perfected his Russian accent and colloquialisms. They would not pick out flaws in his speech.

"What was the name of your farm?"

Hunter did not know of one. He shrugged. "We just called it 'the farm.' "

Agent Konev frowned deeply. "You don't know the name of the place were you worked?"

"We never paid much attention."

"I say you are a German spy."

Hunter remained silent. That was probably what Wayne Nystrom had told them. Based on what Judy had told him about the NKVD, he now expected much worse treatment—maybe physical torture and an attempt to imprison him in a labor camp.

"What is your mission here?" Agent Raskov spoke this time. "Who is your contact?"

Hunter considered his options. Of course, he could withstand substantially greater torture than a human, but he could not afford to have his captors find that out. In any case, the Third Law required that he not allow harm to come to himself.

"Speak, Hunter!" Agent Konev shouted. "Your silence proves your guilt! Now answer us!"

Since Hunter had given Steve the belt unit to trigger the sphere back in Room F-12, Hunter could only escape by means of his own personal resources. That would endanger the welfare of his whole team. He still did not want to take that step.

Suddenly Agent Konev shot up out of his chair and punched Hunter across the table, striking him in the face. Hunter's reflexes gave him plenty of time to see it coming, and he rocked back slightly with the blow. He carefully sustained much of the punch and allowed himself to fall from his chair to the floor, to give the man some satisfaction.

As Hunter slowly got to his feet, both agents moved around the end of the table. Agent Raskov grabbed Hunter under his arms and hoisted him up. At the same time, Agent Konev slammed his fist into Hunter's abdomen. As before, Hunter reacted the way he judged a human would, doubling forward and then falling to his knees, pulling free of Agent Raskov's grasp.

"Let him think about it," said Agent Raskov.

"He needs more convincing, comrade—and this is only the beginning!" Agent Konev struck Hunter in the head with his knee, almost casually.

Hunter obligingly fell over on the floor. He could see only their lower legs and feet now.

"It's been a long night," said Agent Raskov. "At least, let's discuss it outside. Come."

"All right." Agent Konev kicked Hunter with one foot as a parting shot and switched off the light.

Hunter remained motionless until they had left. The door closed behind them firmly and the lock snapped into place. Then Hunter stood up.

The room was completely dark except for the strip of indirect light entering under the door from the hall. The only possible exit for Hunter was the door. Unless he chose to use it, he could do nothing but wait.

16

The next morning, Steve sat with Judy and Jane in their corner of the warehouse with their bowls of hot gruel.

"What are we going to do?" Jane asked. "Are we joining the work brigade today, or what?"

"It's the best way to blend in," said Steve. "If we leave, we might not be welcome back. Judy, what do you think?"

"What's the point of joining the work brigade? Just to wait till Hunter comes back?"

"Yeah, exactly." Steve paused to eat. "If we start running around Moscow on our own, it'll be even harder for him to find us."

"You could . . . you know." Jane tapped her lapel pin. "If we call him after we leave here, it won't endanger these people again."

"But we'll be stuck with nowhere to go tonight," said Steve. "I think our best bet now is to stay with the work brigade and wait for Hunter to come back."

"I'm afraid we'll wait forever," said Judy. "What

if something permanent happens to him? We'll just be sitting around."

"Let's give him another day, at least," said Steve. "That's not very long."

"I agree," said Jane. "If he has to sneak away instead of break out, a day isn't too long to wait."

"So I'm outvoted," said Judy, with a sigh. "All right. I guess it won't hurt a historian to go out with a work brigade and dig ditches for a day. Maybe I'll learn something useful out there."

Ishihara lay motionless on the hard, cold floor, conserving his energy. Wayne slept soundly, using his cloak for padding. In the morning, the sounds of other people rising and talking awakened Wayne. Stretching, he looked around and then sat up.

"Are you well?" Ishihara asked quietly. He sat up, also.

"Uh, yeah. It was kind of a short night, though. How long was I asleep?"

"Six hours and four minutes. Well short of the eight hours recommended for ideal human rest."

"It'll do."

"I see some people in the front are preparing large vats of hot cereal. We shall be fed."

"Good. I'm hungry." Wayne looked around. "What kind of a place is this?"

Ishihara glanced about the room. "If you look carefully, you can see disconnected cables and holes in the floor where machinery was once bolted down."

"Yeah, I see. What does that mean?"

"I believe this was previously a factory. Now all the industrial machinery has been hauled away."

"Why? Something to do with the war?"

"Yes. I think they carried it away from the advancing Germans."

"In case Moscow is captured?"

"Yes, and also to avoid having it bombed."

Ishihara looked around at the crowd, which consisted mostly of women and children. A small number of elderly men were scattered through it. Some people were getting in line for the rest rooms and for breakfast.

"What do they all do in the daytime?" Wayne asked. "Do they have jobs to go to?"

"I have been listening to people talk. This is a work brigade. After breakfast, trucks will take everyone outside Moscow to dig ditches."

"We don't want to waste any time doing that."

"No. However, before we leave, I suggest you eat. We may have trouble finding other food today."

"Yeah."

Ishihara waited where he was as Wayne got in line for the rest room. By the time he had joined the line for breakfast, most people already had their food. He brought his back to Ishihara and started eating.

"I have continued to monitor the NKVD radio traffic," said Ishihara.

"I guess the car must have been reported stolen by now," said Wayne.

"No, not yet," said Ishihara.

"Not *yet*?"

"We still have some time in which we can use the car," said Ishihara. "At least as long as it still has fuel. We should use it while we can."

"We'll use it in more than one way," said Wayne.

"It will lend us an air of authority, won't it? Maybe we can get some information from the guys up at the front table."

"I think I understand what you mean," said Ishihara. "More play-acting?"

"Right," said Wayne. "But you'll have to do the talking, of course. And you'll have to explain why a couple of important people came begging for places to sleep in the middle of the night."

When Wayne had finished eating, he rolled up his cloak and walked with Ishihara up to the front. Ishihara observed the women ladling out hot cereal and the two men standing by the door and decided to approach the men. He stood up straight and assumed a confident demeanor.

"Who is in charge here?" Ishihara asked.

The two men glanced at him in surprise.

"I am the commissar of this facility," said one. He was a blond man of medium height, about thirty years old. "I have not seen you before, comrades. When did you arrive?"

"We came in late last night," said Ishihara. "We are in pursuit of an enemy agent."

The commissar's eyes widened. "You are? Here?"

"No, no. I have not seen him here." Ishihara described MC 4. "Have you seen anyone of this description?"

"No," said the commissar thoughtfully. "Of course, many people are coming and going these days." He glanced at his partner, who also shook his head. Then the commissar looked back and forth between Wayne and Ishihara. "You are . . . NKVD?"

"We are working in cooperation with them," Ishihara said carefully.

"In cooperation with them? What does this mean? May we see your badges?"

Ishihara had worried about this moment. No one had demanded the real agents' badges, but they had expressed their authority with guns and bluster. Ishihara drew himself up stiffly, hoping to bluff the commissar. "You question our authority?"

"Well . . . meaning no disrespect." The commissar hesitated. "I am Boris Popov, comrade. Who are you?"

"We must be on our way, comrade." Ishihara turned abruptly and walked past him, out the door. His hearing detected Wayne's footsteps right behind him. However, he also heard the commissar and his partner following Wayne out the door.

Ishihara did not look back, feeling that his bluff would work better if he showed no concern over the commissar's attention. He led Wayne at a brisk stride down the sidewalk in the morning light and turned at the alley. The commissar's footsteps stopped uncertainly just outside the door.

In the alley, out of sight, Ishihara got into the driver's side. He closed the door and quickly leaned down to pull some of the wires under the dashboard out where he could see them.

"Aren't we going to start the car the same way?" Wayne asked. "I can steer while you push, but I can't push as hard as you can if you're the one who's steering."

"We cannot convince anyone this car is ours if they see us start the engine that way," said Ishihara. "Get in on the passenger side."

"Okay—but what are you doing?"

"The key to the ignition must allow some sort of electrical connection to be made that starts the engine. If I select the correct wires, then I can make the same connection. I think I have them. Please get in."

"Yeah, okay, okay." Wayne hurried around to the other side and slid inside, slamming the door.

Ishihara had carefully stripped the insulation from a couple of wires. He touched the bare metal together and heard the starter whine. When he gave the engine gas, it started up. He shut his own door and backed out of the alley.

"Wow, not bad," said Wayne. "I understand how a robot works, but figuring out these primitive machines at a glance, without a design to go by—forget it."

"Thank you," said Ishihara, stopping in the street and shifting into first gear. "Now we must drive past the commissar so that he can see us driving away."

Ishihara kept his head straight as he drove past the front door of the converted factory, still pretending to have no concern over the commissar and his partner. His peripheral vision, however, told him that both men were still standing there watching them. They did not react outwardly.

"What do you think?" Wayne asked. "Did we bluff them or are they suspicious?"

"I do not know," said Ishihara. "Cars appear to be fairly rare here, so our possession of one is a powerful symbol. However, they are probably still somewhat suspicious."

"Well—you still haven't heard any NKVD alert for finding this car?"

"Not yet."

"That's great. Maybe we can close in on MC 4 before they do. Where shall we look?"

"I suggest factories and military posts. The First Law will drive him to participate with the local people in ways that might help them."

"Okay. How do we find places like that?"

"Big smokestacks can take us to factories that are still functioning."

"For the military, I guess we have to drive back out to the front, if we have enough fuel."

"Yes."

"You're driving. Take us where you think we'll have the best chance to find him."

Hunter remained locked in the room in darkness. His internal clock kept him aware of the passing time. The sounds of voices and footsteps down the hall told him when the day shift arrived for work. He waited patiently, uncertain of what he wanted to do.

Just before noon, two uniformed guards came into the room. Without a word, they took his arms and escorted him out into the hall. At the end of the hall, they took him down a staircase. In the basement of the building, they placed him in a large barred cell with a crowd of other prisoners.

As the metal door clanged shut behind him, he turned to look at the other prisoners. He estimated that he was sharing space with about sixty other grown men of varying ages. Most sat on the cold floor; some had stretched out and a few remained on their feet, leaning against the walls or the bars in the front of the cell. They were dressed in ordinary street clothes. As they looked back at him cautiously, no one spoke.

Hunter knew that the NKVD was primarily concerned with security risks right now, not petty criminals. His companions down here were almost certainly political prisoners on their way to labor camps in Siberia. He felt an immediate urge from the First Law to help them, to save them somehow. Of course, he knew he could not without risking a significant change to history.

Also, he knew that enough contradictory pressure from the First Law could neutralize him completely.

Wayne noticed that Ishihara was pulling the car over to the curb. They had just spoken to their fourth factory commissar. Each one seemed to realize that their car signified government power; they had all been very cooperative. However, neither Wayne nor Ishihara had seen any sign of MC 4, nor had anyone they questioned.

"Why are we stopping?" Wayne asked.

"The car theft has finally been reported," said Ishihara. "We must decide what to do now."

Wayne grabbed the door handle. "Well, let's get going! Come on!"

"Immediate flight is not necessary," said Ishihara calmly. "The description of the car and the plate number have been announced to agents at large over the NKVD radio band, but so far no one has actually reported sighting us."

"Let's keep it that way," said Wayne, grinning nervously. "I mean, why stay in this car until they *do*?"

"I am not suggesting we should. However, I judge that we have some time left to us. The NKVD does not seem to have reported the car theft to the regular city police."

"Well—maybe they reported by phone. That's why you didn't hear it on their radio band."

"I can monitor the city police band, as well. They still have not reported this theft."

"Yeah, I see. What do you think—maybe the NKVD doesn't want to admit it could happen to them?"

"I believe this is the case. They will want to maintain the image of the NKVD as all-powerful."

"What do you suggest we do now?"

"Maybe we should approach a military installation—" Ishihara stopped suddenly.

"What's wrong?"

Ishihara held up his hand for Wayne to wait.

Relieved that Ishihara had not malfunctioned in some way, Wayne waited, watching him.

Ishihara turned to him. "The NKVD has reported a sighting of someone of MC 4's description." Ishihara pulled the car away from the curb and drove down the street.

"Oh, yeah! I forgot—Raskov and Konev are still looking for him, too. Where is he?"

"He was originally reported sleeping in a schoolhouse that had been used for housing displaced citizens. Everyone there is in a work brigade that digs ditches every day."

"You know where?"

"Yes. I have the same directions that were just given to the other NKVD agents."

"Raskov and Konev might be there. They'll recognize us when we drive up."

"As we approach, we can decide how to proceed. In the meantime, I shall continue to monitor the radio band. They will not be able to communicate over it without letting us hear the message, too."

"We're driving right into the lion's den," said Wayne. "But if that's where MC 4 is, that's where we have to go."

Steve, Judy, and Jane joined the work brigade for the day. They rode out to the antitank ditches with everyone else and spent the morning digging together. They moved far enough from the other workers to talk among themselves privately, but Steve did not call Hunter again. He knew that Hunter would not try to contact him, and that left him undecided about what to do.

At midday, they got in line with the others for lunch. After they received hard rolls and bowls of a thin vegetable soup, they sat down to eat by themselves on the top edge of the ditch. The other workers sat with their own friends.

"Have you looked up the ditch that way at all?" Jane pointed.

"Hm?" Judy turned, her mouth full.

"There's a guy up there who's small enough to be MC 4. I saw him just now."

"Really?" Steve tore off a piece of a hard roll. "There must be hundreds of people in the ditch all around us. Where is he?"

"Right now, he's lost in the crowd," said Jane,

leaning to her right as she tried to see him again. "And he was in the distance, almost out of sight."

"I don't see him, either," said Judy, leaning the other way to look.

"How well did you see him?" Steve asked. "I mean, are you sure it was MC 4?" He looked in disgust at his bowl of watery soup.

"Well, no. But he was dressed poorly; his coat was too big and one sleeve was torn."

"Like he might have picked up cast-off clothing from somewhere," said Steve.

"That's right."

"What was he doing?" Judy asked.

"He was digging like everyone else." Jane was still looking up the long ditch, but she shook her head. "I don't see him now."

"Judy," said Steve. "What would happen if we went to look for him?"

"I don't think we should. These brigades are rigidly organized."

"What would happen to us?" Jane asked.

"I don't know. But I don't see anybody walking around socializing." Judy lowered her voice. "It's hard to convey just how oppressive the Communist Party is during this era. Even the military units have party members watching over the ideological purity of everyone. And, of course, they can summon the NKVD at any time to take away dissidents, real or imagined. The same is true right here."

"I'm convinced," said Steve. "We don't want to attract attention to ourselves. Without Hunter here, I don't want to take any unnecessary risks."

"Especially since that guy might just be some-one else," said Jane. "I only got a glimpse."

"Let's just keep looking from here for now," said Steve. "If he does look like MC 4, then at the end of the day, maybe we can see which truck he gets on. That will help us find him later tonight."

"Good," said Judy.

Steve thought a moment. "What are the chances that we would just run into him like this? Doesn't that seem farfetched to you?"

"I suppose it does seem like a coincidence," said Judy.

"It's not just pure chance," said Jane. "Remember, Hunter specifically identified a certain area of Moscow where he expected MC 4 to appear. Our warehouse is nearby."

"That's right," said Judy. "And all the displaced citizens who are not working at something more essential are being drafted into the work brigades."

"Exactly," said Jane. "So his presence here, in a brigade from the same neighborhood as our warehouse, is not really too unlikely."

Steve nodded, looking through the crowd in the distance again. "Maybe we have a chance, then."

Ishihara drove while Wayne sat rigidly next to him. Though Wayne had to be excited by the pros-pect of finding MC 4, a glance at him told Ishihara that his human companion was frightened by the fact that other NKVD agents were going to the same location. So far, they had hardly even left the outskirts of Moscow.

"We're leaving the city," Wayne said anxiously. "What's our route?"

"I have been considering this," said Ishihara. "From what I have been able to observe and over-hear on our travels so far, the Soviet lines are positioned mainly to the north of Moscow. I believe they are poised to make a flank attack on the Germans when and if the Germans advance eastward on the city. The antitank ditches are being dug straight west of Moscow, but still have military patrols behind them."

"And that's where we're headed."

"Yes." Ishihara drove a varied pattern through the west side of Moscow. Finally he found a well-used, unpaved road leading out of the city. They drove in silence.

After the midday break, Judy picked up her shovel and looked again where Jane might have seen MC 4. Then as Judy resumed digging, she worked her way toward a middle-aged woman in her own brigade. Steve glanced at her but merely nodded, trusting her to be careful.

Casually, keeping her head down while she continued to dig, Judy spoke quietly to the other woman.

"Where is that other brigade from? Do you know?"

"What? Which one?"

"The one working right next to us."

The woman looked up at her suspiciously. She was missing a couple of lower teeth. "Why?"

"Well . . ." Judy smiled and shrugged in what she hoped was an embarrassed manner. "There is a man over there I would like to meet."

"Ah!" The woman laughed. "Ah, yes, I see. Well,

they spend their nights in that school near us. You know the one, that was bombed. They had to fix up the roof."

"Uh—yes. It's down the block from us?" Judy did not want to admit how little she knew.

"No, no. It's on the next block."

"East of us?"

"No, my dear. North."

"Oh, yes. I'm sorry."

The woman looked over toward the other brigade. "So which one is he?"

"Well . . . I don't see him right now. He's a rather short fellow."

"Short?" She laughed, shaking her head. "Ah, you're so silly."

They went on digging. Gradually, Judy worked her way back to Steve and Jane. When they were far enough from the others not to be overheard, she told them what she had learned.

"I just wish we could get a good look at him," said Steve. "If we knew for sure it was MC 4, we could make some definite plans. Maybe we could even grab him, take him back, and then return for Hunter."

"Really?" Jane asked. "You'd do that?"

Steve grimaced. "I wouldn't like it much. It's a possibility, but I'm getting worried about Hunter."

Eventually, Ishihara could see the military patrols ahead of them on the rolling steppe. Sentries blocked the road. It was 2:37 P.M.

"Have you decided what you're going to say to them?" Wayne asked.

"I shall say something similar to what we said to the commissar in the factory."

Ishihara slowed the car as they approached the checkpoint. Wayne stiffened visibly in his seat. Ishihara rolled down his window, preparing to speak to the sentries.

Without a word, a uniformed sentry nodded grimly and waved them through the checkpoint. Wayne glanced at Ishihara in shock. Ishihara showed no sign of surprise as he nodded back and drove past them.

"This is really easy," said Wayne, with a sudden laugh. "This NKVD car makes all the difference, doesn't it?"

"I believe part of the reason is up ahead," said Ishihara, pointing. Ahead of them on the same road, another car similar to their own was just moving out of sight in the distance. Ishihara slowed down a little.

Wayne looked. "What do you mean?"

"I suppose that the agents in that car explained what their business was out this way," said Ishihara. "The sentries just assumed we were with them. That is why they felt no need to question us. Even in the military, no one in this society wants trouble with the NKVD."

"But now we have to worry about those other agents," said Wayne.

"I have already slowed down to let them move away from us," said Ishihara.

"What if they saw us?"

"If we find them waiting, I shall turn around the car and we shall flee. However, I do not expect that. I believe that they will be searching for

MC 4, just as we are, without great concern for us."

"But you said that the theft of our car has been reported now. Why wouldn't they check us out?"

"Maybe they will," said Ishihara. "However, they would not expect the car thieves to be following them. Most likely, they expect us to flee at the very sight of another NKVD car. Remember that the alert to find MC 4 here went out to all the NKVD cars. The agents who come here will expect to see each other near the ditches."

"I hope you're right," Wayne muttered quietly.

"I expect so."

Ishihara drove over the next slight rise in the ground. Ahead of them, down a long but very gentle slope, work brigades dug ditches with shovels. The NKVD car ahead of them had turned right and stopped. Two agents had just left the car and were walking toward the nearest work brigade.

Next to him, Ishihara saw Wayne slide down in his seat, covering the side of his face with one hand.

Instead of continuing straight down the slope, which would have taken them close to the NKVD agents, Ishihara turned at an angle. He began driving left down the slope, leaving the road. One of the NKVD agents glanced back over his shoulder at the sound of their car. Then he turned back to his business at hand, uninterested in them.

"Okay so far," Wayne muttered.

Ishihara took the car down to the ruts that ran behind the ditch. The tracks of large truck tires filled the ruts. They had spontaneously carved a rough service road simply by driving up and down here every day.

"I still hear nothing concerning us on the NKVD radio band," said Ishihara.

"Good." Wayne sighed. Then he looked back over his shoulder. "Those agents are out of sight now. You want me to drive? Then you can scan the workers for MC 4."

"Excellent."

They traded places and Wayne drove slowly down the rough road. When Ishihara instructed him to slow down or stop, he did, always nervously looking around for more NKVD cars. Gradually, they moved down the length of the ditch as Ishihara searched the work brigades. The ditch was full of people digging up and down its entire length.

"Didn't the alert identify which work brigade MC 4 was in?" Wayne asked.

"No. It only gave this general vicinity."

"You could radio MC 4 directly," said Wayne. "And tell him that we are from his own time."

"That would merely alert him to the pursuit," said Ishihara. "He would flee."

"That's what I mean," said Wayne. "We might flush him out that way."

"Ah, I understand. You mean, instead of remaining camouflaged, he would reveal himself by running away."

"Maybe. What do you think?"

"It could work if he is in our sight," said Ishihara. "If he is too far ahead of us, or if he was in the other direction when we turned left, then we would not see him."

"Oh, yeah."

"These ditches are very long," said Ishihara, looking ahead. "To protect Moscow from attack, they must be many kilometers long. We have many workers to consider."

"This is as close as we've come so far," said Wayne, shrugging. "Besides, I'm really getting the feel of how to drive this car now." He grinned wryly.

They continued their slow progress down the length of the ditch. The sun was low over the horizon when Ishihara heard the rumble of large trucks behind them, still in the distance. He did not bother to turn and look.

"Looks like quitting time," said Wayne, glancing into the rearview mirror. "Here come the trucks to take people home."

A familiar shape in the distance, among the workers, momentarily slipped into Ishihara's vision and then disappeared again. "Stop," Ishihara said sharply.

Wayne hit the brake and the clutch quickly. "What's wrong? I don't think the truck drivers will care what we're doing here."

"No, that is not the reason. I saw MC 4."

"What? Where?" Wayne stopped the car and leaned toward Ishihara to look.

Ishihara pointed. "I saw him there, but he is not visible now. He is lost in the crowd."

"Did he run away?"

"I do not believe so. He has no way of knowing our identities and was not looking toward us."

Near them, the workers had also seen the trucks coming. They were picking up their shovels wearily and climbing out of the ditch. The crowd was dense, however, and Wayne could not see MC 4 anywhere.

"Maybe we can have him brought to us," said Ishihara. "We do not have to chase him ourselves." He got out of the car and slammed the door.

Wayne got out and hurried around the car to join him. Ishihara saw a man approaching him and waited for him with an arrogant expression. The man smiled nervously.

"Can I help you, comrade?" His voice quivered slightly.

"NKVD," Ishihara said imperiously. "Do you know the code name MC 4?"

"Mm, no, I don't." He shook his head tightly. "I *really* don't."

Ishihara described MC 4.

"Yes, I remember seeing him. He just joined us a few days ago. A real little guy." The man nodded vigorously.

"Have some people bring this man to me immediately. Do not let him escape."

"Yes, comrade." The man hurried back down toward the ditch.

Wayne, next to Ishihara, let out a long breath. "Is he going to help?"

"Yes," said Ishihara. Then his internal receiver picked up another alert on the NKVD radio band. They had been spotted standing outside the car by a pair of agents who did not recognize them. Those agents were on their way for a closer look.

"We must go," said Ishihara, turning and looking into the distance. In the middle of the line of trucks, he saw another NKVD car. It was trying to get around the trucks in front of it, but the slope was too rough in that spot for it to pass them. "Get in the car and start it. Wait for me. Now."

Wayne hurried back to the car.

Ishihara ran down the slope after the man he had just sent to find MC 4. "Comrade, wait."

"Huh? What is it?"

"An emergency has arisen. Tell no one about this man called MC 4. I repeat—no one."

"All right."

"Where does this work brigade spend the night?" Ishihara asked quickly.

The man gave him an address.

Ishihara ran back up to the driver's side of the car. Taking the hint, Wayne slid quickly over to the passenger side. The driver of the other NKVD car honked his horn and waved for the trucks to move out of his way. When the truck drivers could, they slowly worked their way to the side on the uneven terrain.

"It may be a rough ride," said Ishihara. "Hang on. I will search for a place where we can turn back toward Moscow." He took the car forward with a jerk. Some distance behind them, the other NKVD car still honked angrily at the trucks in its way.

"What if they have us surrounded?" Wayne asked frantically. "How do we know which way to go?"

"Only one car has reported sighting us so far," said Ishihara. "I do not believe they saw the license plate on this car. They saw us standing outside the car and must have had our personal descriptions."

Wayne nodded.

Ishihara gripped the wheel hard and drove forward, glancing in the mirror. The NKVD car had finally passed the trucks and was speeding toward them.

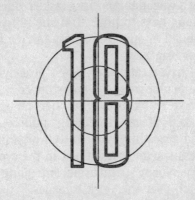

Steve shoveled in silence for the rest of the afternoon. He finally decided to call Hunter again on the ride home, after they had entered Moscow again. Even when the call was intercepted, as he was certain it would be, the movement of the truck through city streets would make locating the transmitter impossible. The NKVD would not be able to focus on a single truck and then hassle the people in his work brigade again. He would just have to be careful about exactly what he said.

The trucks came to pick them up when the sun was low in the west. All the workers began climbing wearily out of the ditches and plodding toward the trucks. Steve glanced around for Jane, then saw Judy quickly working her way toward the neighboring work brigade.

"Come on." Steve grabbed Jane's arm and pulled her after him. He tried to follow Judy, but she had a substantial head start. In the crowd of people moving toward the trucks, the only way he could catch her was to run and dart through the crowd, drawing everyone's attention.

"What's she doing?" Jane asked quietly, hurrying along next to him. "Did she tell you?"

"No, but I'm sure she wants to ride back with the other brigade."

"We'll never catch her. She's already climbing into one of the trucks." Jane stopped.

"I didn't think they'd let her on the wrong truck," said Steve, reluctantly pulling up, also. "She said everything was so well organized."

"I guess she got herself lost in the crowd," said Jane. "Everybody's exhausted, including the guys who watch over the work brigades."

"At least she looks the part enough to do that," said Steve, with a tired grin. "I couldn't."

"We better get on our own truck," said Jane. "Before it leaves without us."

"Come on." Steve glanced one more time at Judy, who smiled at them from the back of the truck she had mounted. He hoped she knew what she was doing. They could not call each other without risking being overheard by locals. At least for now, she was on her own.

Hunter spent the day quietly in the prisoner pen. Very few people spoke and he did not initiate conversation with anyone. They had been fed a tasteless gruel in the middle of the afternoon. Otherwise, the guards merely walked through the corridor on patrol once every hour.

As the hours passed, Hunter considered his situation. At first he expected that the NKVD would eventually take him out and question him further. The additional contact would have brought him new data and allowed him to make more judgments about how to free himself.

However, that had not happened. During the course of the day the NKVD had shown no interest in any of the prisoners. Now Hunter had to consider that perhaps the agents planned no further contact with any of them for a substantial period of time. Theoretically, they might all be shipped to another prison without any more interrogations.

The First Law pressed him internally to help these people. All of them were probably headed for either torture here or a slow death in the Siberian labor camps. Of course, his First Law imperative not to change history took precedence.

However, the internal stress was building. He remained in some danger of being neutralized by the conflict. Finally, of course, he was useless to his team while he simply sat in a cell. Late in the afternoon, he decided that he would have to take action to free himself.

The next time one of the guards came down the hall on his routine patrol, Hunter walked over to the bars. Every other prisoner in the pen was watching to see what he would do. No one spoke.

"I have changed my mind," Hunter said loudly to the guard. "Tell the agents I have changed my mind."

He could hear disapproving murmurs from the crowd behind him. The guard stopped, studying his face suspiciously. Then he came closer.

"You changed your mind?" The guard folded his arms. "About what?"

"I would like to speak to the agents who arrested me," Hunter said calmly.

"Oh, would you?" The guard smiled grimly. "And why would they like to speak with you?"

"I did not answer their questions previously. I am willing to do so now." Hunter, of course, would have to improvise those answers. Right now, his focus was simply on getting out of this pen.

"Maybe you already had your chance." The guard snickered. "Why don't I just let you rot right here? Or maybe I'll just let you freeze. Where you're going, that will be easy." He laughed harshly.

Hunter realized suddenly that the guard was angling for a bribe of some kind. Other prisoners might, from time to time, be able to arrange a bribe through family members or friends. Hunter did not have that choice.

"The agents will be very grateful when they hear what I have to say," said Hunter. "They will appreciate the guard who brought me to them."

"Yeah? How do I know that?"

"I have information about the Germans," said Hunter. "If you do not report that I am willing to cooperate, then one of the guards on another shift will. He will get the credit. Those agents will not like hearing that you delayed my information from reaching them."

The guard studied him without speaking.

Hunter forced himself to smile. "Maybe you will join me in here, comrade."

"The Germans," the guard said to himself, uncertainly. He looked at Hunter without speaking.

"Let him out," called one of the other prisoners. He was followed by a few calls of agreement from others.

Most of the prisoners remained absolutely silent.

"Well, why didn't you say this was about the war?" The guard drew himself up. "Of course I will speak to the agents for you. This is a matter of patriotism."

Ishihara drove as fast as he dared, using all of his faculties to escape the NKVD car behind them. As they rode roughly over the open, frozen ground, Ishihara scanned the terrain with magnified vision. He picked out the smoothest pieces of ground, utilizing his precise eye-hand coordination to steer so that the tires would get the best traction and the clearest path. Gradually, he began to circle back toward the road they had taken from Moscow.

As Ishihara drove, he watched the pursuit car in the rearview mirror as much as he could. He observed that the human driver behind them was not handling the steering over open ground nearly as well. The NKVD agent was not able to hit the quick turns, twists, and shifts of gears that Ishihara could maintain. As a result, the pursuit car bumped and bounced much more severely. Ishihara slowly gained ground, leaving the other car behind.

Behind them, the sun was already down. Through the waning light, he could barely see the unpaved road which he and Wayne had taken to reach the ditches. Some of the trucks carrying workers back to Moscow were visible on it, the beams of their headlights marking its path. Ishihara headed for the road.

Wayne turned to look over his shoulder at the car following them. "Finally! We're leaving them behind now, aren't we? You see that?"

"Yes." Suddenly Ishihara picked up another communication from the car behind them to their colleagues. "They have realized it, too."

"What? What do you mean?"

"Up to now, they had not called for help."

"Really? Why not?" Wayne looked at him in surprise. "What's going on now?"

"I believe they wanted to catch us and take all the credit for themselves. However, they just radioed our position and direction for the first time to the NKVD at large."

"Oh, no!"

"Do not panic. The nearest NKVD cars which have responded are well behind us. They were spread out along the length of the ditches and have not returned to Moscow."

"But Moscow must have plenty more agents! They'll cut us off on our way back to the city."

"They will try," Ishihara said calmly. He knew that Wayne needed some reassurance. Since Ishihara did not have any good news for him, he tried to convey confidence through a calm and reassuring demeanor.

"But what are we going to do?" Wayne asked frantically. "I mean, at some point we'll have to jump in time again. But I still hate to do that."

"The trucks on the road haven't answered by radio; I don't think they have radios. I think we should be able to reach the edge of Moscow without being caught. At that point, we have a chance to get lost in the city."

"But the whole NKVD will be coming for us now, won't they?" Wayne looked behind him again.

"Yes, I expect so. Once we have eluded the immediate pursuit in Moscow, we shall have to plan on abandoning the car out of sight and escaping on foot."

"Okay." Wayne looked at him for a moment, a little calmer now. "Okay. Just tell me what to do."

Ishihara decided not to tell Wayne at this time that he was not sure what to do. Leaving the car somewhere in Moscow was not enough. To escape the current pursuit effectively, without moving through time again, they required a crowd of people in which to lose themselves and shelter for the night.

By the time Ishihara reached the road, the NKVD car following them had fallen well behind. Its headlights bounced crazily in the darkness. Ahead of Ishihara and Wayne on the road, the trucks were roughly a half kilometer ahead.

Ishihara drove in silence, gradually catching up to the ponderous trucks. Since the car pursuing them would soon reach this road, too, and speed up, he passed the first truck. When he could, he passed the next one. Slowly and patiently, he moved to the front of the convoy and eventually faced an open road to Moscow.

In the distance behind them, he soon saw the headlights of the pursuit car swinging around the trucks, also. Soon they were in a simple race on the frozen, unpaved highway. Ishihara drove as fast as the car would safely go, still using the edge that his robotic skills and reflexes gave him. Slowly, they simply pulled away from the car behind them.

When Ishihara came to an intersecting road near the edge of Moscow, he slammed on the brakes and took the turn sharply. The tires squealed and Wayne hooked one arm over the back of his seat to steady himself.

"I apologize," said Ishihara. "But from now on, we are in greater danger, as you mentioned earlier, of being surrounded by the NKVD."

"We have to find a place to abandon the car," said Wayne. "Right?"

"Perhaps not yet. I have the address of the work brigade in which MC 4 was working."

"What? Why didn't you tell me!" Wayne laughed suddenly, a little anxiously.

"I was concerned about escaping the pursuit," said Ishihara. "If we were caught, I did not want to harm you by adding additional disappointment."

"That changes everything! Let's just go get him—if more NKVD guys don't find us first."

"We are on our way now," said Ishihara. "I am taking an evasive route. Now that we have the complex of city streets in which to lose ourselves, I believe we have a good chance of success."

"What about their radio communication—are they going to surround us or something?"

"They are trying already," Ishihara said calmly. "The pursuit car has continued to radio ahead for help. However, as long as they use the radio to communicate and report their positions, I shall know where each of their cars is moving."

Wayne nodded. "Okay. Good."

Ishihara chose not to worry him further by telling him just how close the pursuit had become.

Hunter remained standing by the bars in the prison pen after the guard walked away. He kept his back to his fellow prisoners, hoping to avoid a confrontation. Many of them were muttering angrily among themselves about his willingness to cooperate.

A very few defended his choice to reveal information about the German enemy. He decided not to speak to any of them. As always, he feared that unnecessary interaction might lead to events that would be historically significant.

While Hunter waited for the guard to return and, he hoped, take him back upstairs, he also monitored the NKVD radio traffic. He heard the alerts go out to locate the stolen NKVD car. By now, the NKVD had confirmed to him that the stolen car was being driven by Wayne and Ishihara.

Hunter also noticed that an alert had gone out for someone of MC 4's description. No word of his apprehension had been reported yet. Now Hunter was more eager than ever to escape from NKVD custody.

Finally the guard returned with a partner. Without a word, the guards unlocked the door and escorted Hunter back upstairs to the same interrogation room in which he had been held earlier. They seated him inside and looped handcuffs around a table leg before snapping them closed on his wrists. Then they left him alone again.

The room was reasonably warm, much more comfortable than the prison pen in the basement. The steam radiator was a luxury not wasted downstairs. Its occasional hissing was the only sound in the room.

Hunter felt more confident now, however. No matter what happened in this room, he could arrange his own escape without revealing any robotic abilities to the prisoners downstairs. Getting away was now just a matter of time.

More than two hours passed uneventfully. Hunter heard occasional footsteps and voices down the hall and elsewhere in the building, but he overheard nothing pertinent to him. As he continued to monitor the NKVD radio band, he followed the pursuit of the stolen car. He compared the information from the radio communication among agents and their dispatcher to the map of Moscow and outlying areas stored in his memory. As the pursuit continued, he followed the movements of the pursuit cars. He realized that Wayne and Ishihara were working their way back to the neighborhood where the public housing was concentrated.

Abruptly, he received a direct call on another radio band.

"Steve calling Hunter. Don't respond! Just listen, okay?" Steve's voice on the other band was muffled, and nearly drowned out by the sound of rushing air and a loud, rumbling engine. "I hope you're there!"

Hunter understood that Steve was in a place where Hunter's voice might be overheard if it came over Steve's lapel pin. From the background sounds, he surmised that the team was riding one of the big trucks on the way home with the work brigade. Instead of speaking, he transmitted a clear tapping sound in a repeating rhythm: one, two . . . one—two—three . . . one, two . . . one—two—three . . .

"I read, Hunter! Jane and I are huddling down in one corner of a truck, pretending to talk to each other. Look—Judy took off in one of the other trucks. She's chasing MC 4, but we've already lost sight of her truck in the dark."

Again, Hunter acknowledged his receipt of the message by transmitting the rhythmic tapping.

"If there's any way you can meet us back at the warehouse tonight, we need you! And we've all seen MC 4, so we have a shot at getting him. I'm shutting off again. Steve out."

Hunter felt a renewed urgency. His team was on the verge of finding MC 4, but Wayne and Ishihara were also drawing near. In their most recent mission, back to Germany in Roman times, they had taken the component robot into custody and back to their own time only moments before Wayne Nystrom would have caught him, instead.

The voices he could hear down the hall began diminishing. Most of the people left the building, while a few new ones entered. The night staff, much smaller than the day staff, had started its shift.

Shortly after that, Hunter heard two sets of deliberate footsteps enter the front door and come down the hall. The door to the room opened and Agents Raskov and Konev entered. Both their faces were red from the cold; they still wore their overcoats and fur hats.

"This had better be very important," said Agent Konev. "It had better be more important than what we were doing when we were ordered back here."

"It is very important," Hunter said politely. He waited for them to sit down.

"You have further information about the Germans?" Agent Raskov demanded. He pulled off his hat and unbuttoned his coat. "Do not waste our time. What is it?"

Hunter watched him for a moment without speaking. "It is warm in this room, is it not? Perhaps you would like to be comfortable."

Agent Konev scowled but pulled off his hat and tossed it onto the table. Then he unbuttoned his coat and hung it on the back of a chair. Light from the one lamp reflected off the handcuffs hanging from his belt.

Hunter carefully calculated the moves he could make to escape. Of course, he could not actually harm any humans or clearly display any robotic abilities. However, he could use any ability that he could hide.

"What do you have to say?" Agent Konev glared impatiently at him.

"I apologize for the inconvenience," said Hunter. At the same time, under the table, he quietly pulled one of the links loose between his cuffed wrists. When it had opened wide enough, he unlinked the chain between the two cuffs.

"Get to the point," ordered Agent Raskov.

Without a word, Hunter stood up, in the same motion turning over the table toward the two men. Agent Konev was on his left, and as the table fell over on its side and forced the two agents to jump backward, Hunter reached over and yanked the handcuffs from Agent Konev's belt.

"Hey!" Agent Raskov stuck one hand inside his coat, still backing away.

Hunter could not risk getting shot, which might reveal some evidence of his robotic insides. He quickly jumped toward Agent Raskov and ripped the gun out of his hand. Hunter surreptitiously used his strength to bend the trigger sideways slightly, so it could not be pulled. Then he dropped it on the floor.

Agent Konev was reaching for his own handgun. Hunter shoved his partner hard against him, causing them to fall to the floor next to the radiator. The motion threw Agent Konev's gun hand off to one side. Hunter also snatched his gun away and bent the trigger in the same manner.

Before the two men could get up, Hunter snapped Agent Konev's handcuffs on them, looped around one leg of the radiator. While they pulled and scuffled, not yet realizing what had happened, he searched their pockets for their keys. When he found their handcuff keys, he bent them, too.

Hunter heard footsteps running down the hall toward him, probably in response to the noise of the fight. He stepped to one side of the door and waited for only a few seconds. The door was flung open and two more agents ran inside, past him.

Hunter shoved them both from behind, using their own momentum. They both stumbled against the overturned table. Hunter slipped out the door and ran up the hallway.

A man at the reception desk leaped to his feet when Hunter came into view, but then halted at the sight of him. Hunter threw open the front door and found himself outside on the cold, dark street. He no longer had his winter coat, but for now, he had enough stored energy to function even in this temperature. Without stopping, he turned and began jogging in an evasive pattern, around the corners of buildings and through alleys.

Steve and Jane arrived back at the warehouse without any further discussion of their situation. He was worried about Judy but could not see anything to do at the moment. Once they got off the truck, however, Jane leaned over to him.

"Maybe we can find out where that other work brigade went."

"Yeah? How?"

"I could ask around our own brigade. Somebody will know."

"Let's wait for Hunter. I don't want to attract any special attention to us with a question like that."

Jane nodded.

By now, they were accustomed to the routine. They joined everyone else in line for the customarily bland dinner. Then they returned to their private corner to eat it.

Steve looked up from his bowl, feeling a little defensive. "It's tough just waiting, isn't it? I feel like we should be doing something. But right now, waiting for Hunter to rejoin us really is a good idea, I think."

Jane grinned. "You know, you're getting more levelheaded and responsible all the time."

"Who, me?" He smiled wryly. "Too much time with you and Hunter, I guess."

She laughed lightly and nudged him with her elbow, almost spilling the contents of her bowl.

Steve returned his attention to his own meager dinner. He really liked Jane and in moments like this he wished they could talk leisurely, without the danger of discovery that surrounded them and the urgency of completing the mission safely. Then, as always, his earlier doubts recurred. Their rapport was based on the dangers around them, not on any ordinary friendship.

After dinner, the exhausted work brigade members settled in for the night. Some were still talking quietly among themselves about the anticipated German attack. Steve sat against the cold wall, anxiously waiting for Hunter.

Finally he heard a knock at the front door. Steve and Jane both watched as the guards spoke to the visitor. When they backed up and let him in, Steve straightened in surprise.

Hunter had kept his body unchanged, but his face was longer and narrower than before. Even at his height, no one who had seen his face before would believe this was the same person. Most importantly, he plodded wearily, as though he had just finished a long day of physical labor. He worked his way down the wall toward Steve and Jane.

"I'm sure glad to see you," Steve said with a smile. "I would have thought you'd make yourself shorter, though."

Jane was looking at Hunter carefully. "Hunter, are you okay?"

"I am extremely low on energy," said Hunter. "I did not receive any sunlight from which to recharge my solar cells today. I have been using my stored energy through all of last night, during the day, and now tonight."

"Wait a minute," said Jane. "You can store immense amounts of energy. What happened?"

"You are correct. Until I escaped the NKVD a short time ago, I was using very little energy and still had much to spare. However, I left without my winter coat and had to flee through the city without any insulation. Further, I am conserving my energy for the remainder of the night because I feel we should leave here immediately and make our way somehow to MC 4. At dawn, of course, I will begin to recharge."

"We don't know exactly where to find MC 4," said Steve. "Or Judy."

"We can ask someone," Jane added.

"No need," said Hunter. "Judy called me and told me where she is. But MC 4 is not there."

"What?" Jane asked. "What happened?"

"MC 4 never got on the trucks to return to the city. He slipped out of the crowd and disappeared. She saw him heading westward across the steppe, but it was too late for her to get off the truck. She rode back to the school used by that particular work brigade for shelter."

"So we should start by joining up again," said

Steve. "Or do you want to have us spend the night where we are and start again tomorrow?"

"No, I do not dare risk that now," said Hunter. "Judy does not have your experience with living in other times. Also, we now know something about MC 4's location and direction. Last, I fear that the NKVD may yet come back here searching for me again. They might take you two for questioning this time."

"Then let's get out of here," said Jane. "How should we do it this time?"

"The lights will be turned off in a few minutes," said Hunter. "We can afford to wait that long. I suggest we leave the same way as last time, from that other warehouse." He nodded toward the rear door, then toward the circuit breaker box. "This establishment has the same basic design as our previous residence."

"Good idea." Steve glanced around. "I guess it will work again. But I hope we don't need another shelter. If we keep sneaking out of every place we can spend the night, then pretty soon we'll use up all the public housing."

As Hunter had said, the overhead lights were turned out shortly; leaving only a small table lamp burning in the front. Steve and Jane worked their way across the crowded room and flipped the circuit breaker, while Hunter opened the rear door in the sudden darkness and held it. The procedure worked just as well this time as it had before. In a few moments, the team again ran up a back alley out in the cold, clear, night air.

When they were sure no one was chasing them, Hunter stopped to allow his team members to put their coats on and catch their breath.

"Are you both all right?" Hunter asked. His appearance had now returned to normal.

"Yeah," said Jane, as she buttoned her coat. "Wow, it's cold out here."

"I'm fine," said Steve. "Which way do we go?"

"Please simply follow me. It will be faster and quieter than explaining."

Hunter led them at a brisk walk through the darkened city. He kept to alleys and side streets as much as possible, ducking into shadows on the rare moments when vehicles appeared nearby. When they reached the school Judy had told him about, Hunter knocked on the door.

A tall, stocky man opened the door and looked at Hunter coldly. "We are full, comrade. Sorry." He started to close the door.

"We are not seeking shelter." Hunter grabbed the edge of the door in one hand and held it fast. His tone was firm and authoritative. "Please tell Judy Taub to come to the door."

The guard made one more attempt to jerk the door shut. His eyes shifted to Hunter in surprise when he realized that he could not move it even slightly. He turned and called Judy's name over his shoulder.

Judy, with a big smile of relief, was already hurrying to the door.

"We shall relieve you of your overcrowding," Hunter said, as Judy slipped out past the guard. "Thank you."

The guard slammed the door loudly.

Hunter led his team away from the door, then he turned to Judy.

"You are well?" Hunter asked.

"Sure, I'm fine."

"Good. Since you radioed me, have you gained any additional information about MC 4?"

"No."

"From what you said, it appears that MC 4 is heading for the German lines. Do you agree?"

"Well, I don't know," said Judy. "I saw him running straight west across the steppe, but that doesn't mean he didn't double back later."

Hunter turned to Jane. "As our roboticist, what do you think?"

"Judy, was he running away from you personally?" Jane asked.

"No. He couldn't have been. I didn't reveal myself in any way as someone from our time. Actually, I never even got very close to him."

"Then I think he must be leaving the Soviet lines for reasons of his own," said Jane. "Some new interpretation of one of the Laws of Robotics must have dictated his actions. Otherwise, the Third Law would force him to take care of himself with shelter, which the work brigade offered."

"So something unknown caused him to leave the work brigade for the German lines," said Hunter.

"Yes, that's my best guess."

"I agree," said Hunter. "He may have learned that radio transmission was in use here. If so, he may have monitored the same NKVD radio traffic that I heard. It has told him that he is being sought, though he cannot possibly know why."

"He will find all sorts of humans in the German lines to save from harm if he can," said Judy. "Behind the lines, the Nazis have prisoners of war and political prisoners they have gathered during their campaign."

"The First Law could keep him busy there, then," said Jane. "Hunter, what are we going to do? He could start interfering with history as soon as he reaches those prisoners."

"Those lines are a long way from here, aren't they?" Steve asked. "And he's on foot."

"Yes," said Judy.

"A robot of his type can walk that distance in a night without stopping, though," said Jane. "He would be very low on energy by the time he arrived, but he can count on the sun to recharge him at dawn."

"So, without a vehicle of some kind, we don't have a chance of catching him," said Steve. "He had a head start out at the ditches and now he's been hiking for a couple of hours already."

"I dare not steal a vehicle, as Wayne and Ishihara

did," said Hunter. "I fear it could cause a significant disruption in events."

"Well, we have one more problem now," said Judy. "If my memory serves, the Soviet counter-attack will begin at dawn. Anything we do now will happen during actual battle conditions."

"I see," Hunter said stiffly. "That eliminates any choice of crossing the neutral zone between the armies. I cannot risk that much harm to you."

"You have a plan?" Steve asked.

"Once again, I must make a concession I do not like," said Hunter. "We shall have to return to our own time and then come back to this time, but behind the German lines. Please stand close to me. Steve, please give me the belt unit."

As his team members crowded around him, Steve pulled the unit out of his shirt and offered it. Hunter glanced around to make sure that no local people could see them. Then he triggered the unit.

Wayne finally began to relax as Ishihara drove through the smallest back streets in Moscow to reach their destination. For the first time, they had a real lead on MC 4. Then, without speaking, Ishihara slowed down and stopped the car by the curb.

"Something wrong?" Wayne felt a sinking sensation.

"Yes," said Ishihara. "A new report has just gone out on the NKVD band."

"What did it say?"

"MC 4 is not at the location where his work brigade is spending the night. Some other agents who interrogated people in the work brigades got a lead on MC 4 by using his description, at about the time the brigades got on the trucks to go home. The agents figured out which work brigade he had worked in and reached them ahead of us. I fear that our need to take evasive measures delayed our arrival until it was too late."

"What happened to him?"

"They do not know for sure. Those agents questioned people in the work brigade and reported that MC 4 never got on the truck back at the antitank ditch. They think he may be hiding out in the ditch tonight."

Wayne thought a moment. "Just spending the night there? That doesn't make sense. They'll all be back tomorrow."

"Of course, they believe he is limited by human abilities."

"So we came all the way back to Moscow for no reason? He stayed out there all along?"

"Do not forget that the NKVD spotted us out there. We had to make this run back into Moscow in order to lose the pursuit. It was not wasted time."

"Well—all right."

"I think MC 4 is probably now fleeing back across the neutral territory to the German lines. They know no human would attempt that on foot."

"Yeah! He has to flee the entire Soviet-held territory now. And that means we can still get him first! Even the NKVD won't go all the way to the German lines. Let's go!"

"We can attempt it," Ishihara said calmly. "I must warn you that we have only a quarter tank of gasoline left. We have no money with which to acquire more and attempting to get some by stealth would probably also bring renewed pursuit."

"Well . . . how far can this thing go on a quarter tank?"

"From our driving so far, I estimate that we might reach the German lines. I am certain that we would get within walking distance."

"I want to go after MC 4 now, while we have a chance to snatch him out in open territory. Will the First Law let you try it?"

"Yes," said Ishihara. "The Germans were not exactly happy with us, but they will certainly be more hospitable than the Soviets."

"Then let's go."

Ishihara drove away from the curb.

"We can pick up his trail back at the ditch," said Wayne.

"Our first problem is getting around the anti-tank ditches," said Ishihara. "Those ditches are too deep and steeply dug for this car to cross. There are no bridges or causeways across them; that would defeat their purpose. We shall have to go around one end. Then we can search for MC 4's trail."

Wayne nodded.

"The greatest gasoline expenditure will be another evasive pattern through the city to escape the NKVD's notice. Once we are past the ditches, I can slow down to conserve gasoline usage and still maintain greater speed than MC 4 has even at his fastest."

Wayne said nothing. His earlier elation had been

dampened by the need to reverse direction, but the news was not really that bad. In fact, if they could find MC 4 out on the open steppe with fuel in the car, then chasing him down and grabbing him would be even easier than apprehending him in the middle of a work brigade.

As before, Ishihara took them safely out of Moscow by a long, involved route with many turns. They reached the same unpaved road that they had taken to the ditches earlier. At first, Wayne did not see any other headlights as they left Moscow behind. After a while, however, he saw Ishihara glance into the rearview mirror.

"Trouble?" Wayne looked over his shoulder and saw headlights far behind them, but on the same road.

"Yes, but they are not aware of it yet."

"Huh? What does that mean?"

Ishihara reached out and switched on the car's communication system.

Wayne heard static crackling first, followed by a man's voice speaking a couple of Russian phrases. The man waited, then spoke again. Wayne could not understand the words, but he could tell that the speaker was repeating the same phrases again.

"I first heard him over a minute ago on my internal receiver," said Ishihara.

"What's he saying?"

"He is just trying to get me to respond. It is merely a standard NKVD opening; I have learned that they all use it. He must have recognized this car as an NKVD vehicle, but is too far back to see our license plate. For this reason, he has not yet realized that we are in the fugitive NKVD car. He and his partner are almost certainly going to look for MC 4 at the ditches and he simply assumes that we are doing the same."

Wayne grinned. "Well, we are."

"True. However, I dare not respond. Instead of confirming to him that we are the fugitives, I shall wait for him to figure it out." Ishihara turned off the car speaker again.

"What are we going to do about them?"

"I shall just keep driving. We have a good lead. Once we find a way around the ditch, we shall take off west across the open steppe."

"Okay." Wayne looked back again. The other car seemed to be just a little closer.

Steve felt the same familiar time shift as before. The team suddenly found itself jammed together in the dark, curved bottom of the sphere they used to travel in time. It opened and he could see Hunter climbing out.

"Please remain where you are," said Hunter. "I shall program the console and rejoin you immediately."

"Hold it, Hunter," said Steve. "There's no need to hurry right back, is there? I mean, we can go back to whatever moment we want whether we leave now or in a couple of hours, right?"

"Yes. Why?"

"Well, look. We're all tired and we could use some good food for a change. You're low on energy, and ought to recharge. Then we can return to the German lines in the morning, with our sleep schedule matching their time zone."

"Sounds great to me," said Judy. "Especially

about getting a really nice dinner. Something with dessert."

"Yeah, Hunter," said Jane. "We can split up for now and come back fresh."

"I agree that we should take some time here," said Hunter, as he helped Judy get out of the sphere. "However, I do not want us to leave the Institute. I am concerned that unexpected distractions and unpredictable problems might arise."

Steve jumped out and unbuttoned his coat. "You want us to sleep here? We can do that. What about food?"

"I can help, of course." R. Daladier, the security robot who had been left here originally, was still standing motionless by the door that opened onto the hall.

"I will arrange for Daladier to bring whatever food or personal items you wish from anywhere in Mojave Center," said Hunter. "Steve, after dinner, I suggest you sleep on the couch here. I shall help Judy and Jane find another room with couches elsewhere in the building."

"Sounds okay to me," said Jane, shrugging. "Go ahead and plug into the building's power system to recharge, Hunter."

"I shall do so," said Hunter. "It will not take long. Then I shall arrange different costumes for all of us. We should not wear Soviet clothes to visit the Germans."

"Now, then," said Steve. "What are the choices for dinner?"

Wayne stared forward into darkness as Ishihara drove over rough, frozen ground at the southern end of the antitank ditches. From now on, Wayne knew, they had no road to follow. The car bounced hard, jarring him, and he grabbed the back of his seat to steady himself.

"Are they turning back?" Wayne asked.

"See for yourself," said Ishihara.

Wayne looked back. Now four sets of headlights were following them. The NKVD car that Ishihara had refused to answer over the radio had obviously figured out that they were the fugitives. Other cars had been called and they had converged on the trail.

The chase continued over the open steppe. The car bounced and veered hard; at times Ishihara had to slow down to keep control.

After a while, Wayne looked back again. The pursuers were slowly gaining. Their headlights, too, jumped and jerked in the darkness.

"Why aren't we gaining? When you drove over open ground last time, you left them behind."

"This car has sustained damage from the hard use we have given it. I have to drive more slowly now or else it may not last for the entire distance. The cars behind us have apparently not suffered as much. However, their gain on us has been very gradual."

"Well . . . how far do we have to go?"

"We have covered seven of the approximately eighteen kilometers to the German lines."

"How about this—radio forward to the Germans. They still believe we're German spies, so they should help. What do you think? We can tell them that we're bringing back important information."

"We have none."

"I know, but . . . it might help. We'll think of something when the time comes."

"We still cannot risk precipitating a battle."

"That isn't the Soviet military behind us; it's a bunch of civilian cars. And German patrols must be out this way already."

"I agree. I shall call."

Wayne watched him in silence for several minutes.

"I have made contact," Ishihara said finally. "I explained our dilemma and approximate position to the German radio operator who responded. I also told him we have spoken with Major Bach, whose name may help us."

"You told him we have critical military information about the Soviets, right? What did he say?"

"Yes, I told him. I have been instructed to stand by."

Wayne looked back again. The headlights behind them looked a little bigger than before. "Do you think we're going to make it?"

"I do not know. As I said before, the First Law will require me to take you to another time and place before I allow you to be taken by the NKVD."

"I don't want them to get me, either. But maybe we could just jump forward a few hours. And behind German lines? Not so far into the future that Hunter will grab MC 4 in the meantime."

"It is possible, but we would again have much explaining to do. They would want to know how we got back there, especially without their sentries noticing. We shall have a considerable challenge already in giving them any information about the

Soviet military important enough to impress them but unimportant enough so that it will not alter the course of history."

"Yeah. Just don't make any move unless we just can't get away from the NKVD any other way."

"I agree. Further, I have good news. The German operator has just radioed back. He called the German patrol on duty in this sector. An armored car is coming out to meet us."

"Great!" Wayne glanced again at the headlights behind them. They were closer than ever. "I hope they get here in time."

"I suspect that only our claim to have military information has caused anyone to go to this much effort for us."

"Yeah, well, whatever it takes." Wayne grinned.

"I fear your history is poor. You do not realize just how horrible the Nazi regime was. We run the risk of angering them."

The race across the frozen neutral zone continued. Wayne turned in his seat and watched in horrified fascination as the four NKVD cars behind them narrowed the gap. Slowly, but inexorably, their headlights grew larger. Soon they had closed within three or four car lengths. Then they began to spread out.

"Ishihara—they're surrounding us. They're going to close in."

"I see," said Ishihara. "However, look forward again."

Wayne swiveled. He saw two tiny lights ahead in the distance, bounding over the horizon. "Ishihara! Is that the German patrol?"

"Yes. I have just made contact. It is Leutnant Mohr's patrol again."

"How close are we to the other side?"

"Not very. I estimate we are near the twelve-kilometer mark of the total eighteen."

Suddenly a loud, staccato popping sounded in the distance.

"Hey—are they shooting at us?" Wayne slid

down in his seat. "What's wrong with them?"

"Leutnant Mohr has ordered his machine gun to be fired high over all of us," said Ishihara. "I acknowledged this without objection. It is merely a warning."

"Yeah?" Staying low, Wayne turned again to look at the pursuit. All four cars were veering away from them in sudden turns. "Hey, that's great. They aren't going to challenge outright military power, are they?"

"No."

Wayne grinned. "Wow. That was close."

"Yes. It was. Now we shall follow the patrol back to German lines."

"Do we have enough fuel?"

"I believe so. Just barely."

Wayne sat up, weak with the sudden release of tension. He could see the armored car waiting for them up ahead. As they drew near, it turned and led them back to the west.

After that excitement, Wayne felt profound relief. The remaining six kilometers or so seemed very short now that no one was chasing them. Finally, the armored car led them back through the front lines to a place among the tents.

Ishihara stopped behind the armored car. As the soldiers jumped out of the back, Wayne and Ishihara got out of the car. Leutnant Mohr hurried to meet them, the fur cloak swirling about him in the wind as he spoke quickly in German to Ishihara.

Wayne waited while they spoke. The soldiers in the patrol were attentive, but not hostile. When Leutnant Mohr gestured to a small command tent,

Ishihara nodded and turned to Wayne.

"He wants to talk to us himself. I think he is worried about getting into trouble for coming to get us."

Wayne nodded and followed Ishihara into the tent while the rest of the patrol remained outside. Inside, a soldier sat at a small wooden table in front of a large metal box. Only the antenna told Wayne that it was their crude field radio; the rest of the unit was unrecognizable to him. The tent was a rather meager communications center.

He watched Leutnant Mohr and Ishihara speak in German. As the discussion progressed, Leutnant Mohr became more agitated. Ishihara kept talking, calmly but quickly. Suddenly Leutnant Mohr shouted and the soldiers in his patrol swarmed into the tent to surround Ishihara and Wayne at gunpoint.

Leutnant Mohr gave one more command and the patrol marched out their new prisoners.

Wayne was mystified. Ishihara did not speak, however. They were herded onto the back of the armored car again. This time, the patrol drove them through the lines of gaunt, hollow-eyed soldiers huddling together to the rear. There, they were ordered into a makeshift holding pen.

The pen offered no shelter, being merely a circle of open steppe surrounded by barbed wire guarded by sentries. A crowd of bearded men in ragged and dirty Soviet military uniforms lay huddled on the ground, their only protection from the winter wind coming from each other's bodies. After Leutnant Mohr's men had marched back to their armored car, Ishihara squatted and spoke quietly in Russian for a moment to another prisoner. The other man responded briefly and Ishihara stood up again.

Wayne followed Ishihara a short distance away so they could speak English without being overheard.

"What happened with Leutnant Mohr?" Wayne asked.

"I told Leutnant Mohr about the placement of the antitank ditches. I also told him about the width of the neutral zone between the armies and roughly where I believe the Red Army is placed. I felt I could risk telling him that much, because it will not change the coming battle. Unfortunately, the Leutnant knows that this is worthless information."

"And he got mad."

"Leutnant Mohr feels that we tricked him, which, of course, is actually true. Now the Leutnant has to save himself from Major Bach's anger. I think he is hoping that treating us as prisoners will look good to his superior."

Wayne glanced at the cold, spiritless men in the pen with them. "I would have thought the Germans would have more prisoners than this."

"The man I spoke to here told me that this is just a holding pen for POWs. The vast majority of prisoners have already been marched far to the rear. This pen simply holds those who have been captured since the others left. Apparently, the Germans have a bunch of these small pens up and down the rear of their lines."

Wayne nodded. "Leutnant Mohr overreacted. Don't you think Major Bach will let us out again?"

"Predicting is difficult. Leutnant Mohr is protecting himself when in doubt."

"Well . . . he didn't take my fur cloak away. Last time we saw him, he wanted it."

"Maybe he is simply distracted by larger issues at the moment. I suggest that the time has come to go to another time and place. We could give up on MC 4 and attempt to apprehend one of the other component robots."

"No, not yet. We can always go at the last minute—on the point of death."

"I cannot allow the risk of harm to come that close to you."

"We haven't reached that point yet. Look, you know I haven't done very well. I only need to get my hands on one of the component robots—but I'm desperate for one! I don't dare give up this easily."

"All right. Until more immediate danger threatens, the Second Law still applies."

Wayne nodded, tightening his fur cloak around him. "It's going to be a long, cold night out here."

Steve found breakfast waiting when Hunter woke him. The team ate, showered down the hall, and dressed in the new costumes Hunter had waiting. These clothes looked similar to the previous ones to Steve, but Hunter assured him that the differences in style would be noticeable to the Germans. Then they gathered in Room F-12, wearing new overcoats in anticipation of returning to the Russian winter.

"I see we're all ready," said Judy. "Any final briefing, Hunter?"

"Only that we shall go back to the area behind

German lines, at dawn the morning after we left."

"I was thinking about that," said Steve. "Can't you calculate where MC 4 would be earlier in the night, while he's crossing the neutral zone alone? We could trap him out on the open steppe, without any local witnesses."

"I considered it," said Hunter. "That move sounds easy but it would actually be difficult. For instance, we cannot afford to go back at a time when we were already there; appearing there twice at the same time would risk time paradoxes that could bring about incalculable problems."

"Your internal clock will tell you exactly when we left," said Jane. "You can take us back an hour later. MC 4 would still be out in the middle of nowhere."

"I have no way to predict his precise route. He will probably take some evasive measures, and may alter his path even more as he draws close enough to see or hear soldiers on the German lines. Remember, he cannot just walk up to them without violating the Third Law by getting shot. So as he sneaks up on the Germans, his moves become unpredictable."

"You could still make an educated guess," said Steve. "I like the idea of nabbing him all alone out in the open."

"If I fail to take us within sight of him, we will have accomplished nothing," said Hunter. "We could not risk following him to the German lines."

"I'm with Hunter," said Judy. "We're going back to December 5, 1941. The Soviet army moves on the Germans at dawn. If we're standing between the two armies when it does, we're in big trouble."

"We would have to come back here again," said Hunter. "And go to the German rear anyway."

"Okay," said Steve. "I'm convinced."

Jane nodded.

"Then we shall go directly to the rear of the German lines," said Hunter. "I shall set the console."

Steve helped Jane and Judy climb into the sphere and then followed them. As always, Hunter joined them last and closed it. Steve only hoped they could avoid the dangers of combat once the battle began.

As soon as the team arrived safely on the cold ground, Hunter stood up and looked west in the pale early light. He could not see any sign of the German lines, but when he raised his aural sensitivity, he heard the sounds of vehicles, voices, and marching feet. Then a series of thunderous booms reached them.

"Soviet artillery," said Judy. "The Germans will be moving quickly to prepare for the Soviet advance."

"I do not want to waste any time," said Hunter. "I shall radio in German for help."

Hunter sent out a call in German, identifying himself as a Swiss national whose team was involved with German intelligence. After a brief delay, the radio operator responded that a German patrol would be sent to pick them up. Hunter gave his location as well as he could and signed off.

Soon Hunter could hear the roar of a loud, powerful engine coming toward them.

"I believe the patrol is on the way," said Hunter.

"Probably an armored car," said Judy. "Carrying troops in the back."

"Yes," Hunter said, magnifying his vision and focusing on a speck that had just come over the horizon. "I see it now."

The armored car rumbled over the rough ground as the sound of artillery grew more intense. As soon as it pulled up in front of the team, the soldiers in the back leaped to the ground and fanned out around them, leveling their weapons. One young officer stepped out of the passenger side of the car.

"Hands up! Now!" He was excited, his voice tense. "Who is in charge here?"

Hunter raised his hands and saw that his team also complied. "I am," he said in German as fluent as the officer's. "This man is Japanese; the rest of us are Swiss. We are no threat to you."

"Frisk them!" The officer pointed to two of his men.

As they slung their rifles over their shoulders and trotted forward, Hunter looked at the officer in surprise. "Who are you? What is wrong?"

"I am Leutnant Mohr." He walked up in front of Hunter, studying him carefully as artillery pounded even faster, shaking the ground. "What is your business with German intelligence?"

"We are on the trail of an enemy agent. We believe he may have infiltrated German lines here."

"What does he look like?"

Hunter described MC 4. He was startled to see Leutnant Mohr's face tighten suspiciously. One of the soldiers frisked Hunter and then stepped back.

"They are not armed," he said.

"Take them into the back," said Leutnant Mohr. He turned and walked back to the cab of the armored car.

The other soldiers kept the team covered and herded them into the back. In a few minutes, the armored car was bouncing in a tight circle to return to the lines. No one spoke.

Puzzled, Hunter kept careful watch on all the soldiers. A couple of them held their rifles on their prisoners, but the rest had turned their attention to the booming artillery ahead. Since the shells were not landing nearby, Hunter did not feel that his team members were in immediate danger, but he had to be ready to move if any of the soldiers became more belligerent—and if the shells landed closer.

Hunter had certainly not expected their welcome to be so hostile. At the very least, he had expected his story to be plausible enough to receive some consideration. When Hunter had first heard the tension in Leutnant Mohr's voice, he had guessed that the artillery barrage and the coming battle were the reason. Then he had seen Leutnant Mohr's sudden reaction to MC 4's description. It obviously meant something to him, but Hunter did not know what. All he could do now was wait and look for an opportunity to find out.

Hunter's sensitized hearing brought him more complex sounds of battle every minute. The steady rumble of thousands of tanks now mixed with the heavy pounding of artillery. Over the German radio band, men were shouting orders all along the lines.

Hunter did not take his eyes off the soldiers around him and his team, even when the armored car pulled up to a large barbed wire pen. The soldiers opened the back and jumped out, gesturing for the team to follow. Then the soldiers hustled them through the gate and left them inside the pen. A few men inside glanced at them, but most gazed to the east, where billows of gray smoke rose over the battlefield.

Steve stumbled into the pen, repeatedly shoved from behind by one of the soldiers. As soon as they had locked the gate behind him, however, he saw that the team was together and unhurt. Right now that was good enough.

"Hey, Hunter," said Steve. "Look at the crowd in here. Maybe MC 4 is in here someplace. What if they grabbed him when he showed up and just threw him in?"

"Just as they did with us," said Judy. "That's a good possibility. We should look."

"I am looking," said Hunter. "However, the crowd is dense. Everyone is standing together. I cannot see most people well enough to recognize them." He turned to his team members. "We can move into the crowd in a moment. First I want to say this. I fear we may have to return again to our own time. If the artillery shelling comes near this area, I shall have no choice. So we must remain close together."

"Maybe we really messed up," said Judy. "A big battle in the industrial age is no time to look for

MC 4. I thought we'd be talking to some officers, not just locked up and abandoned."

"Me, too," said Jane. "Hunter, do you want to go right back and pick another time? In all this confusion, I doubt anybody would notice if we just vanished again."

"I agree with you about that," said Hunter. "That gives us slightly greater flexibility. We can afford to wait a little longer before giving up."

"You mean you want to stay longer?" Steve was startled. "Why?"

"The continuing danger is that Wayne Nystrom will beat us to MC 4, even in the midst of the battle. However, my greatest fear is that MC 4 will be hit by gunfire or something worse, damaging him to the point of being unrecognizable. That will make locating him very difficult—perhaps impossible. Coming back after the battle could be useless, and we would never be able to reassemble Mojave Center Governor."

"I don't see what we can do here," said Judy. "And if MC 4 gets blown into junk, then he won't change history."

"You forgot about that nuclear explosion," said Steve. "Even if he's in two thousand pieces that just lie around under the soil undisturbed until our time, we know his remains explode when the time comes."

"Oh—yeah." Judy nodded tightly.

Hunter turned to her. "What happens here today?"

"Let me think. The Germans are on the defensive. They're about to experience their first defeat on the Russian front. During the next six weeks, they'll be driven back until they can stabilize the line in mid-January." She shook her head.

"What's wrong?" Hunter asked.

"Today in particular, I just don't remember much detail. The Germans obviously get the worst of it." She hesitated. "Half a million prisoners in their control, like these right here, will die in the first three months of winter from exposure."

Steve could hear the sounds of artillery and tanks drawing closer. The weapons of this time required that the battle would be fought at a fairly close distance. The ground shook with the thundering of artillery.

"Let's walk up and join the group," said Hunter. "If we're lucky, MC 4 is right here."

The other prisoners had little interest in them, as they continued to watch the smoke rising in the distance. The team slowly merged into the crowd. Hunter, because of his height, could see much more clearly than his team members. When Steve saw motion off to one side of the pen, outside the barbed wire, he turned to look.

A troop of German infantry was marching a long line of other prisoners past the pen, away from the front lines. As the filthy, ragged prisoners streamed past, a German officer stopped at the gate to their pen. The guards nodded and opened the gate.

"Hunter," Steve said quickly, tapping him on the arm. "Look."

Hunter turned. At the same time, one of the guards blew a whistle and began waving for everyone to come out. Another guard began barking orders.

"Judy, what are they doing?" Hunter asked. "Where are they taking all these people?"

"All the POWs are being marched to the rear right away, so they can't be a threat of any kind in the day's operations. These guys were probably held in other pens similar to this one."

Steve watched everyone. The crowd of prisoners around them was already moving toward the gate. Since the marching prisoners were being taken west, away from the growing battle, none of the prisoners in the pen hesitated.

"We shall go with them," said Hunter. "Long enough to find out if MC 4 is here somewhere, or in that other group. If we see no sign of him, we can return to our time and plan again. At least we are leaving the combat behind."

Steve nodded. He waited patiently as the crowd shuffled forward, slowed by the bottleneck at the gate. Again, Hunter led the way and Steve brought up the rear.

At the gate, some prisoners had been pulled out of the line by men in different uniforms. These prisoners were standing at gunpoint just to one side of the gate. Hunter passed out of the gate, as did Jane. Then one of the guards grabbed Judy's arm and jerked her aside, out of the line.

Before Steve could respond, another guard leveled his rifle at Steve and sharply moved the point toward Judy. Suddenly moving very cautiously, Steve stepped over to her.

Hunter turned and saw them from outside the barbed wire.

"Hey! What are you doing with them?" Hunter demanded.

One of the guards slammed the butt of his rifle into Hunter's abdomen. The big robot, unhurt, bent forward slightly at the impact, pretending to react. "Why are you keeping them?"

"They're going to execute us," Judy shouted through the wires.

"Shut up, Jewish pig," said one of the men, spitting on her. "All you subhumans will be eliminated before we go."

Steve slammed into him, knocking him off balance. "Judy, run! Get outside the gate!" He pushed her forward. Hunter could not take the team back while local people stood among them, within the range of the sphere, or else he would take them, too.

Suddenly, in the line of prisoners marching behind Hunter to the west, Steve saw MC 4, his head down like the others. Steve pointed. "Hunter! There he is!" He started to yell MC 4's name, then realized that it would alert the component robot to the pursuit. So far, in the noise and confusion all around, MC 4 had not realized anyone was concerned with him.

Something hard slammed into the back of Steve's head and his legs crumpled, dropping him to the frozen ground with a thump. For a moment, he was dazed. He heard shouts and felt the pounding of feet on the ground around him, but could not think clearly.

Wayne and Ishihara had both seen Leutnant Mohr's armored car pull up to the gate. Wayne had hoped the Leutnant was coming back for them. When Wayne had seen Hunter and his team, of course, he and Ishihara had hidden in the crowd of prisoners. They stayed behind Hunter as the prisoners moved toward the gate of the pen.

Now, however, they had both been herded close to the gate with everyone else. Ahead of him, Ishihara had almost reached the opening. Wayne remained caught behind the bottleneck, near Steve and Judy and the guards holding them. Then Wayne heard Steve shout and point to MC 4, who was about to march right in front of the gate among the troop of prisoners.

Wayne felt a rush of excitement. He, too, pointed to MC 4. "Ishihara, grab him!"

Ishihara was still trapped in the crowd, however. As they shuffled forward with everyone else, Wayne heard a uniformed man tell the woman whom Steve had called Judy that he was going to kill her, Steve, and the others who had been taken aside. Then the man spat on her.

Wayne was shocked. Somehow, until this moment, the people around them had been sort of abstract, unreal. He knew that the combat and stress of war was horrible, but he had not expected to see prisoners simply executed out of hand like this. For the first time, he realized how ignorant he was of this time and these people.

Hunter had moved just outside the gate and beyond the barbed wire, but he responded instantly. Flinging aside one startled German guard, he plunged directly into the barbed wire, stretching it forward with his weight, ignoring how it tore into his clothes. He reached through the wires for Judy and Steve, but two more guards threw themselves on him, forcing him to turn and fight them off.

In the same instant, Ishihara pushed people away from him just inside the barbed wire. He slammed into the guard who had spit on Judy, knocking his rifle to the ground. The immediacy of the danger to people from his own time had forced Ishihara to act under the First Law.

The other prisoners quickly drew away from the gate, hoping to avoid getting hurt if the Germans began firing their weapons. Suddenly the open gateway was in front of Wayne. MC 4 was only a few yards away.

Wayne looked back at Hunter and Ishihara, who were struggling with a knot of German guards and other soldiers. More soldiers had gathered around them with their rifles aimed. They hesitated to shoot for fear of hitting their own comrades.

Steve pushed himself up, stumbling into a standing position. Judy took his arm to help him up. She frantically pulled him toward the open gate.

The angry, impatient guard who had spit on Judy had drawn his sidearm. With deliberate care, he raised it toward the back of Judy's head.

Forgetting MC 4, Wayne threw himself against the man's legs. The gun went off, firing into the ground. Both men fell, tripping some of the troops who had been shuffling in a crazed huddle with Hunter and Ishihara.

Steve blinked, staggering dizzily, and looked around. Judy was dragging him by the arm. Ishihara flung German soldiers away from himself. They fell against the semicircle of armed soldiers surrounding them. Some fired as they went down, but their bullets went wild into the air.

As Judy pushed Steve out the open gate, Ishihara threw himself on the ground over Wayne, protecting him. Then he reached into his tunic, apparently the same one he had worn in ancient Germany. Wayne and Ishihara vanished.

Jane had grabbed MC 4's arm and was trying to pull him after her. He was not coming, but she had slowed him down. Hunter hurled the soldiers around him to the ground just as Steve and Judy reached him. Then Hunter stretched out one long arm and yanked MC 4 closer. Jane came with him, still holding the small robot's arm. Steve saw Hunter reach inside his heavy overcoat.

An instant later, Steve found himself back in the familiar, crowded darkness of the sphere. No one spoke while Hunter opened it, jumped out, and pulled MC 4 into Room F-12 after him. Judy got out next; this time she and Jane had to help Steve climb out slowly. He was still dizzy.

"Hunter, Steve needs to be checked by a medical robot," said Jane. "He's hurt. I can't tell if it's serious or not."

"I am radioing for one now," said Hunter. He turned to MC 4. "Can you hear us speak?"

"Yes."

"Jane, please give him direct instructions."

"Do not make any attempt to get away or shut off your receptivity to our instructions under the Second Law," Jane said, looking over her shoulder. "Stay right where you are until we give you further orders. Acknowledge."

"I agree," said MC 4.

Jane turned to Daladier, who still stood by the door. "Do not allow MC 4 to leave our custody. If he makes some interpretation of the First Law to justify it, he might still make an attempt to escape."

"Acknowledged," said Daladier.

Steve sank onto the couch. His head throbbed painfully, but he could think more clearly now, and followed the conversation around him. "Did we leave right in the middle of everybody?"

"Yes," said Hunter. "However, I believe that in the crowd and confusion, with the battle coming near, stories of our disappearance will not be taken seriously."

"The sad truth is, most of those prisoners died soon afterward in captivity," said Judy. "Their stories about our disappearance, if they told them, had nowhere to go but to each other."

"The German soldiers and guards may have lived to tell the story," said Jane. "A few of them, anyway."

"Some may have survived to talk about it," said Judy. "Under the Nazi regime, I feel that anyone who said he lost custody of prisoners who vanished magically would not be taken seriously—he might even be punished for offering such a flimsy excuse. In a system that thrives on fear, the soldiers might have chosen not to repeat what they saw."

"Our concern is a real one," said Hunter. "If possible, we must not disappear in front of witnesses during future missions."

"How did we happen to come across MC 4?" Steve muttered, looking up at him.

Jane turned to MC 4. "Tell us how you came to be a prisoner of the Germans."

"I attempted to sneak up on the German lines and move past them," said MC 4. "However, dawn was breaking by the time I had crossed the open territory and German sentries saw me. They trained their weapons on me and the Third Law required that I not take risks with them. They put me in a prison pen without interrogation. Then some soldiers came and began emptying each pen. They escorted us with weapons and told us which way to go. We marched from one pen to another down the rear of the lines until we reached the one where you were."

"Lucky for us," said Steve.

"Actually, chance factors were quite low," said Hunter. "Under the pressure of impending combat, the Germans were imprisoning all strangers and marching them together out of the area. We were all caught in the same net. If we had not spotted him when we did, we would have had to return to our own time. However, in a later trip to complete the mission, we would have still have found him in the group marching to the rear."

"What do you think?" Jane grinned at MC 4.

"I agree."

"Steve," said Hunter. "How are you feeling?"

"I think I'll be okay."

"With your permission, I shall contact the medical robot again and have him meet us at MC Governor's office. Are you well enough to ride there?"

"Yeah."

"Daladier, please remain here and continue to watch for Dr. Wayne Nystrom and R. Ishihara," said Hunter.

"Of course."

"Jane, please instruct MC 4," said Hunter.

"You will remain with us as we move through Mojave Center to the office of MC Governor," said Jane. "You will still cooperate with us fully and make no attempt to escape us or to interfere with our return to the office."

"Acknowledged," said MC 4.

Hunter led his team out. Steve gratefully allowed Jane to take his arm and support him. Hunter had a Security detail waiting to drive them back.

Outside the office of MC Governor, a medical robot was already waiting for them, holding his small black case of equipment.

"I am R. Cushing," said the medical robot. "My patient is named Steve, I have been told."

"That's me."

Cushing stared at Steve for a long moment. "My specialized vision reveals no fracture. You will be fine." He took a pressure gun from his black case and held it against the side of Steve's neck. It popped against his skin. "This is a mild painkiller. My infrared vision tells me that the inflammation is localized and stable. For the swelling, I recommend that you apply ice."

"Okay," said Steve. "Thanks."

"I shall leave you," said Cushing. "I am permanently on call, so contact me if the situation changes. I do not expect it will."

"Thank you," said Hunter.

Cushing departed.

Jane came up and gave Steve a quick hug. "I always knew you had a hard head."

Judy walked up on the other side and gave him a hug, too. "That guy clobbered you after you knocked down the one who spit on me. He was about to shoot both of us. I'll never forget that."

Steve smiled wryly. "I won't either."

"I feel so bad about Ivana, too," said Judy. "She was totally helpless, and completely innocent. I wonder what happened to her."

Jane gave Judy a quick hug. "Whatever it was, it happened to her long before we ever went back and met her."

Judy nodded.

"Those two regimes have disturbed me deeply," said Hunter. "The earlier societies we have visited were primitive in their values because of their early place in social evolution. However, the Nazi regime and the Soviet Union were barbaric throwbacks. Their values were more primitive than those of many societies which had preceded them."

"And they had the power of the industrial age to use in their atrocities." Judy straightened, her voice firm.

"It's fairly old history now," said Jane.

"And the obligation of our time is to remember it," said Judy. "The larger lesson is that technological development does not necessarily mean civilized values—we all have to remain on guard. Humans, unlike robots, have the power to choose how to behave."

Everyone was silent for a moment. Then Judy shrugged, smiling self-consciously. "Well, end of lecture. Look, I want to clean up. Okay if I excuse myself?"

"Of course," said Hunter.

"I'll say good-bye a little later," said Judy. She slipped out.

"We haven't asked you about the nuclear explosion yet," said Jane. "Hunter, I suppose you've been monitoring the news since we returned."

"Yes. No explosion has taken place in Moscow."

Steve looked up. "I feel better already. That stuff Cushing gave me works fast."

"I have news of another nuclear explosion, however," said Hunter. "I checked the sphere console before we left Room F-12 and the information matches. The current unexplained nuclear explosion has eliminated the city of Beijing, the capital of China. Millions have died already."

"China?" Steve grinned. "On our next mission, I'll be the one who fits in for a change."

"What time in history will we visit this time?" Jane asked.

"The time of Kublai Khan, when he was Emperor of China."

BIO OF A SPACE TYRANT
Piers Anthony

"Brilliant...a thoroughly original thinker and storyteller with a unique ability to posit really *alien* alien life, humanize it, and make it come out alive on the page." *The Los Angeles Times*

A COLOSSAL NEW FIVE VOLUME SPACE THRILLER—
BIO OF A SPACE TYRANT
The Epic Adventures and Galactic Conquests of Hope Hubris

VOLUME I: REFUGEE   84194-0/$4.50 US/$5.50 Can
Hubris and his family embark upon an ill-fated voyage through space, searching for sanctuary, after pirates blast them from their home on Callisto.

VOLUME II: MERCENARY   87221-8/$4.50 US/$5.50 Can
Hubris joins the Navy of Jupiter and commands a squadron loyal to the death and sworn to war against the pirate warlords of the Jupiter Ecliptic.

VOLUME III: POLITICIAN   89685-0/$4.99 US/$5.99 Can
Fueled by his own fury, Hubris rose to triumph obliterating his enemies and blazing a path of glory across the face of Jupiter. Military legend...people's champion...promising political candidate...he now awoke to find himself the prisoner of a nightmare that knew no past.

VOLUME IV: EXECUTIVE   89834-9/$4.50 US/$5.50 Can
Destined to become the most hated and feared man of an era, Hope would assume an alternate identify to fulfill his dreams.

VOLUME V: STATESMAN   89835-7/$4.50 US/$5.50 Can
The climactic conclusion of Hubris' epic adventures.